CROOKED CREEK

Raiders are terrorizing the buffalo range, wiping out hunters' camps. 'Notso' Wise, a former Texas Ranger, is recruited to bring the thieves to justice. Doubts exist that the local lawmen are pursuing the raiders with sufficient vigour, and Notso doubts he has the subtlety the job requires. The raiders are led by Jim Hardiman, a ruthless villain who uses a network of informers, backed up by cold-blooded murder. Has Notso got what it takes to bring him down?

GREG MITCHELL

CROOKED CREEK

Complete and Unabridged

LINFORD
Leicester

First published in Great Britain in 2013 by
Robert Hale Limited
London

First Linford Edition
published 2015
by arrangement with
Robert Hale Limited
London

A catalogue record for this book is available
from the British Library.

ISBN 978–1–4448–2249–6

Published by
F. A. Thorpe (Publishing)
Anstey, Leicestershire

Set by Words & Graphics Ltd.
Anstey, Leicestershire
Printed and bound in Great Britain by
T. J. International Ltd., Padstow, Cornwall

This book is printed on acid-free paper

1

On Crooked Creek the working day was ending in the buffalo-shooting camp. The herd that Joe Long and his men were hunting had moved away and the shooters had enough hides to fill a large wagon. The last of the skins had been salted, folded and stacked under a tarpaulin. Tomorrow they would load the wagon and return to Woodville.

The crew had washed as well as they could in the creek, the cook was building up the fire and banging his cooking utensils while the sound of a bell indicated that the horses and mules were hobbled and grazing peacefully.

Long had already poured boiling water down the barrels of the three new Sharps rifles the company had sent. The black powder used in the big cartridges left a corrosive residue that had to be removed. He was cutting patches from an old flannel shirt, which he would push through the rifles' bores to dry them. When a man made his living by shooting, only a fool would neglect his tools of trade.

From the darkening trees that lined the creek a disturbed bird took flight. Two years ago that might have been a sign of trouble but the army now had the Cheyenne and Arapaho hunters corralled on reservations.

A jangling bell from the direction of the stock suddenly indicated some other movement, more urgent than grazing, and the hunter laid aside his work and stood up. He was more curious than alarmed, but then one of the skinners called his attention to the creek bank.

'Someone's at the creek.' If the man intended to say more, he never got the chance.

Dark figures emerged from the trees with repeating rifles spitting flame and murderous lead.

* * *

Stiff from a long coach journey and burdened with a heavy saddle and tightly packed saddle-bags, Jeff Wise was glad that Waldron's office was not far from the stage depot. As he studied the neatly lettered sign on the building's front he could not help thinking that Sam Waldron had done pretty well for himself since he left the Texas Rangers.

Entering through a glass-panelled door, he found himself confronted by a severe-looking, middle-aged lady at a desk.

Florence Gower tried not to show the disapproval on her face but sometimes she did not approve of the company that her boss kept. The young man before her had made some sort of effort to look respectable but the saddle on his shoulder and the ivory-handled Colt on his hip were sure indicators of a lack of social standing. To Florence's mind, respectable young men were behind counters in banks, railroad stations or shopping emporia.

'Can I help you?' she said in a voice that challenged the newcomer to say that she could not.

'Sam sent for me. My name's Jeff Wise.'

'Just wait here, Mr Wise. I'll see if Mr Waldron is available. You can put down that saddle. I have no intention of stealing it.'

Wouldn't know a good saddle if she saw it, he thought as the lady disappeared through the door behind her.

'Notso!' Waldron's voice boomed out through the open doorway. 'Get in here, you mangy young coyote. I expected you a damn week ago. I was starting to think you got hung for horse stealing. What kept you?'

Wise had been finishing the education of some broncs on a big Texas ranch when Waldron's message reached him, but he did not expect the latter to be interested in excuses. He smiled his thanks to a plainly disapproving Florence, who was not quite sure that Sam was joking, and entered the small office. A smell reminiscent of burning dog hair told him that Waldron was still addicted to his ancient pipe.

His former sergeant was there, thicker in the middle, thinner on top and looking older than he had in his ranger days. A plaster cast was on the lower left leg, which the older man was resting on his desk. He indicated a chair. 'Put the weight on your brains for a while if you haven't had them all shaken out bronc-busting.'

'At least horses don't shoot back. I've been enjoying a peaceable life but I have the feeling that you're about to spoil that.'

Waldron leaned forward and drew his shaggy eyebrows down as if to shade his hard blue eyes. 'I have a job for you if you're interested. It pays a hundred a month and expenses.'

'Sounds to me like you're looking for a hired gun, Sam, but unless you've changed I don't reckon you'd be in anything like that. What's this all about?'

'I'm offering you a job as a detective. I'm partners with a former Pinkerton man named Abrahams and we've set up our own agency. He handles the Eastern end and I handle all the West. When I heard you had left the rangers I decided to track you down, because I have a job that would suit you just fine.'

'I can recall being on some other 'just fine' jobs with you, Sam. I have the scars to show for them. Remember that little dust-up we had with them Comanche raiders and that shoot-out with the Koster gang?'

Waldron raised his hands palms outward in a calming gesture. 'Take it easy, Notso. Detective work is not like ranger work, where you just go in shooting. This calls for a more subtle approach. You use your head more than your gun.'

'Are you sure you have the right man for this? Ain't you forgetting that I am called Notso Wise?'

'You were the youngest one in our ranger company and the boys were only teasing you. They couldn't very well call you Mighty Wise or something like that.'

'I don't see why not — but keep talking.'

Sam explained as he stuffed his large pipe with tobacco. 'I have been hired by Collis and Co, hide dealers. They have grubstaked some buffalo-shooting outfits to meet some big Eastern contracts. Trouble is, though, that the teams are getting wiped out and the hides stolen. I was going to take this job myself until a bumble-footed horse fell on my leg and broke it. The company wants to find out who is behind these crimes and what is happening to their hides. I figured you would enjoy a nice ride out on to the buffalo range.'

'What's wrong with local law officers?'

'There's a jurisdictional problem. The ones here are really only town policemen and the extent of their powers is somewhat hazy. The hide-hunters are crossing territorial and state boundaries and no sonofabitch seems to want to take responsibility for what's happening on the buffalo range. Then there's the fact that some local law officers are the best men that money can buy. The hide pirates seem to know every move we make. It's hard to tell who's honest and who ain't.'

Notso leaned forward in his chair and said, 'So I'm just needed to go out there, find these badmen and start killing them till they stop?'

'No. I want you to see what you can find and report back to me. I'll have the proper legal authorities notified when it's time to act. You don't have to shoot anyone unless they need it real bad.'

'I don't think much of the buffalo trade,' the younger man said. 'I don't have a buffalo rifle and I sure as hell ain't taking on a skinner's job. So just what do I tell folks I'm doing if they meet me on the range?'

'There's plenty of mustangs out there. You can say that you are looking the herds over with a view to rounding up a few. You always did spend too much time with horses and can sound mighty convincing when you start talking about them.'

Notso frowned and shook his head.

'That story sounds a bit weak to me. We need something more than that. Does this town have a local newspaper?'

'Yes, a weekly, comes out the day after tomorrow. What do you have in mind?'

'Some folks have already seen me come in here and it's easy to make a connection with you that brands me straight away as a lawman of some kind. What about putting an advertisement in the paper offering a big reward for a valuable stud horse that's been lost on the open range? Describe a fictitious horse with a fictitious brand and offer a reward big enough to interest a footloose fella like me. That would give me an excuse for staying out on the buffalo range. There's always a few mustangs hanging about the buffalo because they like the same feed.'

'I reckon I could do that,' Sam said. 'I can give you the money for a horse and any supplies you need but you can travel light. I'll give you a note to Joe Long. His shooting outfit is working for

9

our client, Collis and Co and is operating along Crooked Creek. He'll supply the grub and let you use his camp as a base. You can get a horse from Tony Garcia, who has a barn further down the street. He trades horses and has some pretty good ones at times. Our client is paying the bill, so pick the best you can.'

'I sold my Winchester before I came here; didn't think I'd need it. Do you have a spare I can borrow?'

'I haven't but you can take my old Sharps carbine. It still shoots well and has more reach than a repeater. I doubt, though, that you will be getting into any shooting scrapes. Detectives have to be a lot more sneaky and rely on their brains more than their guns.'

'I remember those Sharps carbines didn't always shoot true once the barrels got hot.'

'Remember that,' Sam grunted. 'Try not to shoot too often. Use your head.'

Notso smiled. 'With my name are you sure I am really right for the job?'

'You'll have to do.' Sam laughed. 'There's not a lot of likely talent here in Woodville. I'll give you a rough map that will get you to Crooked Creek. Follow it upstream and you'll find Long's camp somewhere along it. Now book into Reed's Hotel, get some rest and start getting your outfit together. If anyone asks you about me, just tell them I hired you to look for a valuable horse that's been lost. As you leave, tell Florence to come in and we'll get started on that fake ad.'

Though he did not know it, Notso's visit to the agency office had already been noted. Within minutes of his booking into the hotel his name was known; it did not take a genius to guess that a man carrying his saddle would soon be heading for Garcia's barn. The watcher knew who he was and could give a good description of him. He was also aware that Notso had some connection with Sam Waldron. He would make a few more enquiries and, if necessary, would send a word to Big Jim. The latter would decide whether the stranger should live or die.

Notso dumped his few belongings in the hotel room and decided to get himself a horse before relaxing. Remembering situations where horses were needed in a hurry, he always rested easier knowing that a good horse was readily available.

Tony Garcia was a small, bow-legged Mexican with the narrow eyes of a shrewd dealer. He showed Notso a couple of fairly ordinary mustangs and could see immediately that his prospective customer was not impressed. When Notso asked if he had something better, Garcia produced the black mare.

She fitted the prospective purchaser's requirements perfectly. Standing fifteen and a half hands, five years old and beautifully proportioned, the mare was the ideal type for what Notso had in mind. The Mexican produced a saddle and bridle and, at Notso's request, saddled the animal. 'Would you like to see her ridden?'

'Yes. Just ride her around a bit and if

she seems to be moving right I'll try her out.'

The mare moved well. She was range-raised and a little jumpy in town but her mouth was good. After riding her, Notso was happy to part with fifty dollars of the Waldron agency's money. Horses were cheap at the time but he still considered himself fortunate to have purchased such a quality animal so inexpensively.

'I'll collect her tomorrow,' he said. 'Does she have a name?'

'*Sí señor*, she is called Snowball.'

'Ain't that an odd sort of a name for a black horse?'

Garcia smiled and parted the mare's thick forelock. A round white spot on her forehead was her only marking. 'There, *señor*, is the snowball.'

Notso laughed and patted the mare's neck. 'It's not such an odd name after all. It's a change to find a black mare that's not called Bess. I think I have a good one here but if I find something wrong that you should have told me about, I'll be right back.'

'I am sure you will be pleased with this one,' Garcia confidently told him.

The distant watcher had seen enough. The stranger would not be long in Woodville and, despite his cowboy clothes, he had the look of a lawman about him. It was time to warn Big Jim.

2

Big Jim Hardiman was named for his criminal influence rather than his physical build. Of average height, middle-aged, tubby and balding, he did not look particularly dangerous, but few who underestimated him survived for long. Though his skill with his long-barrelled Colt .44 was only average, it was a foolish man who took him cheaply. At almost any time he could call on the services of some deadly and ruthless henchmen. They were loyal to their boss because he was smart, had the knack of making money, and paid well. Big Jim's main skill however was in the way he manipulated his crew. He appealed to their greed, vanity or ambition, secretly playing one against the other, making it easy to destroy any who might be a threat to his leadership or to the safety of the gang.

He was camped in a grove of cottonwood trees on a slight divide that overlooked miles of open country. In the middle distance to the south the winding course of Crooked Creek was advertised by the trees growing along its banks. Hardiman would have much preferred to camp on the creek, but his present location was a better vantage point. If anyone was approaching he could not afford to be caught by surprise.

A messenger from Woodville had ridden half the night to advise him that a man, likely to be a detective, could be headed his way over the next day or so. That was a development Hardiman had not been expecting. With Waldron out of action and Fritz Heimer, the town sheriff, reluctant to get involved, he thought it was time to get more ambitious in his plundering. More time was needed and the best way to gain it was to eliminate anyone who interfered.

Willie Prentice was loafing in the shade with Creek Johnny his half-breed partner. Neither would think twice about killing a man and they were unlikely to ask too many questions. A hard-faced pair of nondescript appearance, the only clean things about them were their guns. Each wore a pair and Creek Johnny also sported a large Bowie knife.

Big Jim called them over and told them that they were to watch for a rider likely to be headed for Crooked Creek. He was young, dark-haired, medium-sized, wearing range clothes and sporting a white-handled Colt. He would also be riding a black horse.

'What do you want us to do if we find him?' Prentice asked.

'Question him and if you find he's a lawman, kill the sonofabitch.'

'What if he ain't the law?'

The boss thought for a while. 'Unless he's someone you know you can trust and might be useful to us, kill him anyway.'

'That's why I like workin' for you, Jim.' Prentice chuckled. 'We never have to do anything too complicated. It's

17

hard to recall a problem that we haven't fixed with hot lead.'

'I remember one,' Creek Johnny said seriously. 'I fixed up an *hombre* on the Red River with my knife.'

'You can reminisce all you like when you're on your horses. Now, get going and don't come back until you've stopped that stranger or are sure he ain't headed this way.'

⋆ ⋆ ⋆

Notso left Woodville at a time when only a stray dog saw him depart. Snowball was feeling fresh and was eager for more exercise, but her rider held her down to a fast walk. He did not want the mare bucking because he had a strong suspicion that she might have been pretty good at it. She had been suspiciously cheap for an animal of such quality. He suspected that she had unloaded someone who had pushed his luck too far but, as with a fighter, it was hard to know how good

18

a bucker was without knowing the ability of the person they had beaten. After the first mile he warily increased the pace, but by then his mount had relaxed and was happy to take orders.

Miles of open grassland glistening with early-morning dew stretched ahead of them. Though the town had been left behind, the white man's handiwork was still very much in evidence. It took the form of rotting carcasses, sometimes a few together and at other times singly. They provided food still for buzzards and various other carrion-eaters. In other places bleached bones showed that Indians and carnivorous animals had been taking their toll on the herds long before the white man arrived, but the old skeletons were few compared to the more recent ones.

He did not expect to see any live buffalo because hunting pressure was pushing the herds south and west. The hunters with their powerful long-range rifles were relentlessly following. Now only bones and circular wallows showed where the great beasts had so recently grazed. Notso had never been fond of the hide trade and, by the scale of the slaughter, he knew that the majestic buffalo herds were doomed. Also doomed was the nomadic life of the Plains Indian tribes.

He pushed such gloomy thoughts to the back of his mind and set out to enjoy the freshness of the morning, the pleasure of having a good horse and room to ride.

When far enough from town he dismounted and set about testing his horse's attitude to gunfire. Holding her firmly by the reins, he fired a shot at a distant group of buzzards feeding on a carcass. As expected, the mare pulled back but was firmly held. She snorted at the smell of the powder smoke but her reactions were only what most horses would do.

He spoke a few soothing words to her and fired again. She threw up her head and snorted but made no serious effort to escape. After a third shot she moved closer to him as though he was her protector. Aware now that she trusted him, Notso mounted and fired another shot. Snowball fidgeted but did not take fright. He dismounted again, reloaded his gun and heaped praise on the mare before mounting once more. She knew then that gunfire would not harm her and thus her actions would be more predictable if lead started flying.

On two different occasions he sighted distant bands of mustangs. They had stopped grazing when they saw the rider, watching him suspiciously, ready for instant flight if he approached them. He was glad to see the two small groups, as they gave some credence to his story about searching for a missing horse.

They made good time to Crooked Creek and Notso let the mare quench her thirst, then graze a while on the creek bank with the cinch slackened and the bit out of her mouth. A drink of water and a couple of the biscuits he had brought from town would have to suffice for a midday meal. He would have a decent dinner when he found Joe Long's camp.

★   ★   ★

Prentice and Creek Johnny were following the creek, keeping away from the open plain and staying in the timber as much as possible. Notso, who had just resumed his journey, saw no reason for concealment and was riding in the open when the two riders came out of the trees about a hundred yards ahead of him. His appearance caught the pair by surprise but the way both went for their guns plainly demonstrated a lack of peaceful intentions.

'Stop right where you are!' one rider bawled and spurred his horse forward. His partner quickly did likewise.

Notso wheeled his mount and rode hard for the trees on the creek bank. A gun fired as he did so and he heard a near miss whizz past him. If nothing else it confirmed that his instinctive flight had been a wise decision. He needed to get under cover quickly and he charged in among the trees. Too late he saw a loop of Crooked Creek, with high, steep banks, immediately in front of him.

Before he could choose a course of action the black mare made up her own mind. She launched herself over the creek, almost leaving her startled rider behind. Notso glimpsed the brown water below him, then the mare landed lightly on the other side. He was thrown forward and caught the saddle horn with his ribs but almost instantly regained his balance.

Fifteen feet would not worry a trained hunter but it was a long jump for an untrained, range-raised animal. Neither of the pursuers' horses would face the jump and the cursing riders lost ground as they sought an easier creek crossing. By the time they found one, their quarry was a quarter of a mile ahead.

'He's gettin' away!' the half-breed

shouted. But he was wrong.

With time to think, Notso decided that he had run far enough. At an old buffalo wallow he reined in the mare and dismounted. A second later he had loaded the Sharps carbine. This weapon had a flick-up peep-sight screwed to the metal tang holding the stock to the action. Peering through the small aperture he picked up the galloping riders, laid the foresight on the man in front and squeezed the trigger.

The heavy carbine roared as it slammed against his shoulder and the mare jerked back in alarm, almost pulling the reins from his left hand. But through a cloud of powder smoke he saw that the leading horse was now riderless.

Creek Johnny hauled his mount to a stop and slipped from his saddle. Prentice was moving feebly in the grass and the amount of blood on his shirt front showed that he was badly wounded.

'Willie . . . ? How bad are you hit?'

If Prentice heard him he made no reply, or it was drowned out by another shot from their intended victim. The bullet missed only because the nervous mare had jerked Notso's arm just as he fired.

Aware that he was facing a single-shot weapon, Creek Johnny dragged a Winchester repeater from its saddle scabbard, hoping to fire before his opponent had reloaded. But by the time he had the rifle to his shoulder Notso was again in the saddle, and riding hard. He was almost at the limit of the repeater's accurate range and there was no time for proper sight settings. The half-breed aimed high with what he hoped was the correct amount of elevation and fired. The shot missed.

With his intended victim apparently in flight, Johnny turned again to his fallen comrade.

But Notso had no intention of fleeing. Coming to a slightly rising piece of ground, he dismounted again, moved the rear sight to 400 yards and sighted on the tiny red dot that was the half-breed's shirt. It was a long shot for any sort of open sight but well within the Sharps capability if he could point it right. This time the mare did not pull back and the man in the red shirt appeared to go down.

'Now,' he said to Snowball, 'we'll amble down there and see who those two unsociable cusses are.'

He was readjusting the rear sight on the rifle when he saw the red-shirted man appear from the long grass, struggle into his saddle and gallop away. The other rider's loose horse tried to follow but became entangled in the fallen reins and was making little progress. The retreating rider appeared to be half-lying on his mount's neck, as though badly hurt, so Notso decided that he would not pursue him. If his comrade was still alive he would be a more likely source of information.

A cautious approach was unneces-sary, because as he came nearer Notso could see that the man was dead.

The mare snorted nervously as her rider dismounted but followed on a slack rein as he led her closer. To his surprise, Notso knew his victim. He was Willie Prentice, a Texas outlaw whose misdeeds were recorded in the Texas Rangers' book of bad characters.

'I wondered where you'd gotten to,' Notso said to the dead man. 'I'm also mighty curious as to what you were doing here on the buffalo range. Too bad you didn't live a bit longer, Willie.'

3

Notso moved quickly, searching the dead man for any personal belongings and removing his guns and cartridge belt. He caught the loose horse, unsaddled it and turned it loose again. It was probably a stolen animal but he had more important tasks in mind and did not want to be hampered by the extra horse. The slicker rolled behind the cantle of the dead man's saddle proved a handy wrapper for the Winchester carbine and the other armaments. It was easy enough to find a spot to hide them among the rocks and low bushes on the creek bank. He saw no point in leaving the weapons where they might be used against him at some later date. He covered the dead man with the saddle blanket and placed the saddle over his face as a temporary deterrent to scavenging animals. Then he remounted his horse.

Scarcely half a mile further along the creek he picked up the tracks of wagons and horses. They were easy to follow and if Sam's information was right, they would lead to Long's buffalo camp.

* * *

Creek Johnny, despite a deep bullet graze in his thigh, rode hard. He was lucky to be alive and knew it, even if later he had to face the wrath of Big Jim. They had both made the fatal mistake of underestimating their intended victim, but at least he could tell his boss that someone who was not afraid to swap lead was in their territory and that someone was probably a lawman.

Hardiman swore long and hard when he heard the news because he thought that he had bribed or scared off most of the law's guardians in the area. After ordering one of the gang to tend the half-breed's wound he paced around the camp with a frown on his face and murder on his mind. He did not know much about the new player in the game but was sure that he had to die.

He was unaware of the newcomer's destination but reckoned it was best to check on the one place that had to remain undiscovered for at least another few days.

Creek Johnny was his best tracker, but he would not be riding anywhere for a while, now that his wound had cooled and his leg had stiffened. Tracking was out of the question but Big Jim would get his man by guessing at his movements.

'Roy,' he called to a tall, skinny youngster in a fringed buckskin shirt, 'you and Johnny stay here and watch the camp. The rest of us are goin' after that sonofabitch that killed Willie.'

Roy would have preferred to go with the others, but a recent scar on his eyebrow was a reminder that it did not pay to argue with Big Jim.

Fred Ennis, a huge bear of a man with a greystreaked beard, was tightening the cinch on his horse when he asked his boss, 'Where are we going, Jim?'

'We're goin' to Long's camp because I reckon that's where that *hombre* with the black horse is headed. But even if he ain't and we meet him on the way, we kill the sonofabitch.'

★   ★   ★

Joe Long's camp was not what Notso had expected. There were no wagons or livestock or hides. No campfire was lit, although the day was nearly over and it was only the circling buzzards that had attracted his attention. Riding closer with an ever-increasing feeling of dread he saw the reason for the buzzards' presence. He counted five dead men sprawled untidily in positions indicating sudden death. Their pockets had been turned out and a couple of men were minus their boots. Hoof marks, boot tracks and wheel marks had churned up the ground. A large square of dead grass showed where a stack of rolled,

31

salted hides had been stored and a short distance away the blackened ashes and partially burned wheels showed that a wagon had been burned. Those who had plundered the camp had left clear tracks leading to the northwest.

Notso dismounted and studied the remains of Long and his crew. All had been shot several times and three had been shot in the back. Copper casings from .44 rim-fire cartridges showed that a couple of the attackers had used Henry or '66-model Winchester repeaters, not weapons favoured by the buffalo trade because of their low power.

He checked the burned wagon in case there was another victim. Mostly it was just a pile of blackened wood but one wheel had only been partially burned. Traces of yellow paint still remained on it. Then he realized that there were only three wheels among the ashes. Even if one had been totally consumed its iron tyre should still have been there. Looking around he could see no sign of the missing rear wheel.

The shadows were lengthening and Notso knew that it would soon be too dark to follow up the tracks of the wagon and the killers. He mounted Snowball and rode a short distance to ascertain the general direction the hide pirates had taken. Not far from the camp he found a broken rear wheel from a wagon and the distinctive square mark caused by the base plate of a wagon jack. The raiders had taken a wheel from Long's wagon after one of their own had collapsed. The necessary repairs and the loading would have taken several hours' work and it brought him no comfort to realize that the killers might not have been as far away as he had first thought.

A snort from his mare caught his attention. She was standing with ears pricked and head high, looking along the creek. Before he could stop her Snowball neighed. Another horse immediately replied.

Notso peered into the gathering gloom and saw a dark mass of riders moving parallel with the creek. They were barely 300 yards away and had started to pick up their pace.

He vaulted into the saddle, kicked into his stirrups and urged the mare out onto the open prairie. Behind him he heard raised voices and pounding hoofs. It had been a long day for Snowball but she was well-bred and he hoped she had the necessary staying ability to keep ahead until darkness afforded some protection.

Someone behind him fired a shot, but only an optimist could hope to hit a target hundreds of yards away from the back of a galloping horse in poor light. Notso's biggest fear was not of being shot, it was the fear that his mount might fall on the rough ground. Open grasslands are never as smooth as they appear to be, with many holes and other obstacles invisible in the fading light. A couple of times the horse jumped objects that the rider never saw, and that was some comfort. She was not running blindly but watching where she was going and greatly reducing the risk of a fall. But it would be a long run back to the safety of Woodville — too long at the rate they were going.

Darkness found Notso still ahead but the gap had diminished as Snowball tired. Visibility was limited and the night promised to be moonless, but the chances of his horse falling were increasing. Somehow he had to shake off the pursuit long enough to give the mare a temporary rest.

Barely visible in the gloom, he sighted ahead an even darker mass, indicating a large patch of trees. Thinking that they might offer some concealment, he urged his mount towards them. It seemed a sensible course of action, although one that the pursuers would expect. Then an idea came to him and he decided to take a risk.

As soon as he reached the first few young trees on the edge of the forest, he halted, jumped from the saddle and held down the mare's head. She was glad to stop and now was in no mood to neigh.

Their cover was flimsy but the plan worked. Sure that their quarry was headed for the dark trees, a party of horsemen came racing past barely fifty yards from where Notso was standing. None even thought to look sideways. Allowing the pursuers a couple of minutes to get into the forest, he quietly led the horse out onto the open plain. The hunters would be busy for some time, blundering around in the almost total darkness and quickly becoming disoriented. The chance of their firing upon each other by mistake was a distinct possibility, but no shots were heard as Notso moved away from the scene. Only when the trees were lost in the darkness and Snowball had regained her normal breathing did he mount again. But he still kept at a steady walk in case the hunters were somewhere close enough to hear a galloping horse, for sounds carried long distances on such still nights.

An hour later they were quenching their thirsts on one of the many loops of Crooked Creek. Notso unsaddled the mare, rubbed her back and staked her out on his lariat to graze in a grassy patch among a few cottonwood trees. Then, with his gun in his hand, he stretched out on the ground and almost immediately fell asleep.

Without a groundsheet the earth was soon damp and cold so he did not sleep long, probably only a couple of hours, but it was some rest. The mare had managed a bit of grazing but Notso had nothing to eat and hunger added greatly to his general discomfort.

Walking to the edge of the trees, he looked out across the prairie. Miles away he saw the tiny gleam of a campfire. He guessed that the hide pirates had stopped for the night, but he knew they would be scouring the landscape when daylight came.

It took a great effort of will to force himself to wait another hour, just to give his mount a bit more rest. He walked about, for a while sat uncomfortably with his back against a tree, even stretched out on the damp ground, but he could not relax. When the sun came up he would be visible as he crossed the open grassland and he wanted to be as far away from his enemies as possible. He had only a vague idea of the direction of Woodville, but he would be able to get his bearings when the sun rose. Then, the shorter his route to safety the better he would like it.

He looked towards the tiny speck of light that was the campfire. Aloud he said, 'Sleep well, you mangy pack of coyotes, and sleep as late as you like.'

4

The first glimmer of the rising sun gave Notso the directions he needed and he wasted no time getting into the saddle. Alternately trotting and cantering, he soon left Crooked Creek behind but kept an eye to the north-east, where he had seen the fire through the night.

A couple of times he sighted distant bands of mustangs, and in one place an ugly little roan stallion came trotting up, tossing his head and prancing in an effort to lure the black mare away. Then, as if satisfied that his charm had not worked, he wheeled away and trotted back to the rest of his band.

Notso judged that two hours had passed when he saw the first riders. There were two of them, tiny specks to the north-west but headed in his direction on a course that would intercept his. Their course was an unexpected one but he had no reason to believe that they were friendly. His first impulse was to dismount and try a couple of long-range shots with his rifle but, just on the chance that the newcomers were harmless, he decided to hold his fire until they made an aggressive move. The strangers were holding their horses to a brisk walk and seemed in no hurry. Suspiciously he watched and, as the gap between them narrowed, he noted something unusual about the nearer rider.

The person who sat astride a large bay horse was small and wore a colourful pink shirt such as no self-respecting cowhand would wear. Long blonde hair showed beneath a black hat, and what Notso at first thought were chaps turned out to be a brown, divided riding-skirt.

'Hell,' he said to his horse as if it might have been vaguely interested. 'That's a girl.'

Her companion was a tall, skinny individual clad in rough working clothes with the look of a homesteader about him. His horse was tall, dark brown, of a similar type to the girl's. Notso was not able to see if he was carrying a gun but he had seen enough badmen in his ranger days to guess that this man was no gunman.

Reassured, Notso turned Snowball in the direction of the approaching riders, neither of whom appeared concerned by the meeting.

As the distance closed Notso could see that the man wore a gun but it was high on his right hip in a tight holster and not situated for a fast draw. With that matter resolved he turned his attention to the girl. She was young and pretty, despite the frown she was wearing.

He tipped his hat to her. 'Howdy, folks. Out for a morning ride?'

'You could say that,' the man said quietly as he cast a wary eye over him. 'What about yourself?'

'I've done all the riding I want in these parts and I'm heading back to

Woodville. I suggest that you do the same too. There's bad trouble around here.'

The girl said suspiciously, 'Things look quiet enough to us. You would not be trying to scare us off, would you?'

'Why would I do that?'

'Maybe you are frightened that we will catch that valuable stud horse that the big reward has been offered for. My brother and I know we are not the only ones looking for that horse. I think you might be the man who left town yesterday. Tony Garcia told us about you.'

Notso laughed. 'You sure picked me right. I'm Jeff Wise, more often known by disrespectful folks as Notso.'

'I'm Cyrus Hall,' the man said. 'This is my sister, Clair. It seems we are business rivals. We're after the same horse as you are. Tony told us about the missing horse and the big reward last night just before we were leaving town to go home. A dark-brown stud horse, about sixteen and a half hands with a double triangle brand on its shoulder, should be easy to spot among the mustangs around here.'

The girl said, 'The reward is open to anyone, so we feel that we have as much right as anyone else to try to claim it.'

'You sure have. The trouble is that I am pretty sure that horse ain't around here. That's partly why I'm on my way back to Woodville.'

Unsure whether he should tell them about Waldron's fake ad that had worked a little too well, Notso dodged that issue. Instead he told them, 'Now's not a good time for horse-hunting. Yesterday I found a buffalo-shooting camp wiped out and their hides stolen. The killers chased me yesterday and are probably on my tracks now. I think we should all ride back to Woodville, and the sooner the better.'

'You must think we are green to fall for that story, Mr Notso,' the girl told him coldly. 'With us out of the way you could double back and get that horse all for yourself.'

'Forget about that horse. There's hundreds of mustangs around here and you could look for a month without finding it. I'm not trying to trick you. This place is dangerous. If you run into those killers you won't have a chance. They are travelling slowly with a big load of stolen hides and they won't want the news getting out too soon. They've already killed five people. Come back to town with me.'

'You'll excuse us, Mr Notso,' the girl said, 'but we are not that dumb. We'll take our chances with those killers of yours and we won't be back in town until we are leading that missing horse. Things are mighty tough on our homestead at present and we need that money.'

Cyrus was looking beyond Notso and silenced any further argument. 'Just hold your horses a minute, Sis. Look behind you, Notso. There's three riders coming this way and they're not wasting much time about it.'

Wheeling his mare around, Notso

saw three riders like specks in the distance, but they were moving quickly, growing larger by the second. 'Looks like the ones I was warning you about,' he said. 'Now maybe you'll believe me.'

Notso drew the carbine from its saddle boot, dismounted and set the rear sight at 400 yards. He depressed the trigger guard and pushed a big cartridge into the open breech. 'I suggest you folks get going. I'll slow them down for a while but then I'll catch up with you mighty quick.'

'I'll stay with you,' Cyrus volunteered.

'You only have a revolver and I don't intend letting them get in range of that. Those cusses are riding much better horses than those harness horses that you and your sister have. If it comes to a race, they'll run you down quickly. Your horses with that draught in them might have a short burst of speed but they can't stay. Now quit arguing and get going. Our friends over there are nearly in range.'

Notso squinted through the sights. The oncoming riders were still small targets and there were long odds against hitting them, but he knew he could go close and hoped that the riders might be bluffed into holding back when confronted by long-range fire.

A rider on a grey horse was the most visible, so he concentrated on him. The Sharps kicked hard when he fired but he saw the rider jerk up his horse's head in alarm and knew that the bullet had gone close. There was just time to load in another cartridge and snap a shot at a big man on a sorrel horse who was now the closest. The horse went down as though its legs had been swept from under it; the rider had not been thrown clear. The third rider, whether by a desire to help his friend or lack of nerve, hauled his mount to a stop beside the fallen horse and called to the man on the grey. Having lost one horse before they were even in Winchester range, the killers decided to reconsider their strategy. As they came together Notso sent another bullet their way. It missed, as he'd expected it would, but served its purpose in warning the others that they could be shot down before they were even in a position to retaliate.

With his message delivered, Notso mounted his horse and cantered after his new acquaintances.

* * *

Ennis managed to get his leg from under the dead horse and struggle to his feet. Favouring a badly bruised leg, he shouted to the man on the grey horse. 'Get back to Big Jim. Tell him what's happened and that there's three people to stop now. They're headed for Woodville so he can still cut them off if he hurries. Get another horse out here for me, too.'

Nate Masters watched his companion ride away, then asked Ennis, 'What do you want me to do?'

'Hang around here. The two of us

will discourage that sonofabitch from comin' back and shootin' me from long range.' Ennis was not sure whether they were facing a superior rifleman or a lucky shooter, but he knew that a misjudgement could have fatal consequences. He saw no point in pushing his luck at that stage.

Notso looked back and saw the man on the grey riding hard from the scene; the purpose of his errand was easy to guess. The two Halls were half a mile ahead, holding their horses to a fast trot, sparing them as much as possible because they had a long ride ahead. He did not push his mount too hard and it was a while before the three were reunited.

'What happened back there?' Cyrus asked.

'Nothing much. I shot one of their horses and they suddenly developed a respect for a long-range rifle. But it looks as though one of them has gone for help. We'll need to be careful.'

'But we're a long way ahead of them

now,' Clair argued.

'They know that we are headed for Woodville and I reckon they've been around here long enough to know a few shorts cuts. This open country gives them plenty of room to move.'

Cyrus looked nervously about. 'Do you think we should pick up the pace?'

'No, just go steady like you are. Those harness horses aren't built for long, hard runs and they can't keep it up for long, but held at a steady pace they can cover a lot of ground. You were a bit ambitious taking this pair out to chase mustangs.'

'They are the only horses we have on our farm, and that stallion is a broke horse, so he might not be too wild,' Clair explained. 'We had hoped that if we took things quietly, Cyrus might be able to get close enough to drop a rope on him.'

Notso, still unsure whether he should tell them the truth about the missing horse, thought it better to conceal the true situation for a while longer. Instead he tried to say something positive. 'Your idea might have worked if you could find that horse, but right now he is the least of our worries. Until those hide pirates are wiped out it won't be safe for anyone out here on the buffalo range.'

5

Big Jim reacted quickly as he always did when trouble threatened. He sent a rider out to Ennis and Masters with a spare horse. After delivering the animal the same man was to locate the hide wagons and tell them to make all speed to the railhead at Simpsons Creek. There the stolen hides could be stored in a warehouse and shipped out a few at a time on east-bound trains. The demand in the East for buffalo robes was strong and the army was buying buffalo coats and overshoes for winter campaigning. Every untanned, salted hide was worth at least ten dollars and Big Jim had stolen hundreds. A tannery in Illinois was waiting for them and many had already been shipped.

He would take the rest of his men and try to shortcut the fleeing trio. Ennis and Masters would be coming from the south to prevent them doubling back. As the gang mounted, he selected a wiry little man whose specialty was long, fast rides.

'Isaac. Get to Woodville as quick as you can and tell our man there what's happenin'. That lazy sonofabitch might soon have to earn the money I'm payin' him.'

★ ★ ★

Notso and the two Halls had managed to leave the open prairie behind and had moved into the foothills of a mountain range that separated them from Woodville. It was a mixed blessing. They would no longer be highly visible but the brush and boulders on the hillside made it much easier for their enemies to set an ambush if they had managed to short-cut them.

A fairly well-worn trail wound over the hills but Notso hesitated to use it. Although there were only the tracks of the Halls' horses on it he knew that smart killers did not advertise their presence and most likely would have approached from a different angle.

'Another hour and we'll be home,' Clair told Notso in a much-relieved tone. She was gradually losing her suspicion of his motives.

'I reckon it will take a mite longer. That trail don't look too safe to me.'

'We didn't waste time and I am sure that if we are being chased at all, those people would be a long way behind us.'

'There's whole cemeteries full of folks who thought that way. We're safer if we move off the trail anyway and take to the brush. There'll be tracks in there made by mustangs and wild cattle. We'll pick up one of those and follow it. Those murdering skunks will only be watching the main trail. They can't ambush us if they don't know where we are. Even if it takes us another hour, going the long way gives us a better chance of reaching safety.'

Clair remained unconvinced but Cyrus agreed with Notso. By nature he was as deliberate as his sister was impetuous. 'It's better we lose an hour or so, Sis, than getting caught up in a gunfight.'

Notso took the lead riding parallel with the hills for a fair way before picking up a narrow trail made by mustangs. Then he turned and followed it up the hill. The path twisted and turned but gradually took them higher until they reached the crest of the range. Remaining under cover, they dismounted and rested their horses.

In the distance they could see the cluster of buildings and the odd smoking chimney that marked Woodville. A few dark-green pines were scattered around the town but from the foot of the hills to the town's limits the landscape was fairly open. However, Notso still had the feeling that all was not well. He looked along the ridgeline in the general direction of the main trail. There, on the reverse slope, he discerned a group of horses among the trees. They would be invisible to anyone who approached from the other side of the slope. He could see no riders but knew they would be there somewhere.

'There are horses hidden over there near the trail. It looks like our friends are waiting for us. We'll keep under cover and stay well away from the trail when we descend the hill.'

'They'll see us when we get onto the open ground,' Cyrus observed.

'By then we'll be too far away for them to do us any harm. I hope that some of those b — ' he remembered Clair's presence just in time, 'have been lying out on hot rocks in the sun and are gradually frying.'

★   ★   ★

An hour later, one of the ambushers took his eyes off the trail and wiped a sweaty forehead with his sleeve. He glanced casually to his right and saw the tiny figures of three riders move out on to the plain below.

'Jim,' he called. 'They've gotten past us. They're down there on the plain.'

Big Jim rose stiffly from his ambush position, looked to where his associate was pointing and, in his usual fashion, swore loudly and long.

'Do we go after them?' one man asked eagerly.

'No, we wouldn't catch them now. We can send someone in after Isaac gets back from talking to our man in town. There might be a chance to get the one on the black horse. He's a detective, and from what we have just seen, he's pretty smart, but that don't mean the sonofabitch is bullet-proof.'

* * *

Sheriff Fritz Heimer was opening the latest batch of mail to arrive at his office. A big man with grey hair and a huge moustache, he was long past his prime. Simple tasks were becoming harder and the ageing lawman knew that his days in office were numbered. He had adopted a mainly administrative role and left the rough-and-tumble work to his two younger deputies. He was tired of peace-keeping and knew it to be a thankless task. Lately the job had been feeling too much for him: he had been at it too long. He knew that secretly Jack Carter and Gus Saunders were more than a little critical of his lack of action and that both deputies were counting the days to his retirement. He supposed that Carter would take his place, but the town council would have the final say there. The older of the two deputies was efficient and well versed in legal dos and don'ts that were gradually seeping into the local law scene. He was a good man with guns or fists, and the town's few troublemakers had quickly learned to steer clear of him. His taciturn nature won him few friends but he was good at his job.

Gus Saunders was younger, more sociable and with an air of boyish enthusiasm. He was acutely conscious of his responsibilities and sometimes looked askance when he saw his boss drinking on duty. The sheriff was carrying a lot of old injuries and the occasional sip of whiskey made the days less painful — or so he said.

Though he got on well with Sam Waldron, Heimer was a little uneasy that another form of law had established itself in his domain. He had never liked detectives and private agencies were high on his list of dislikes.

Most of the day's mail was routine, but an envelope addressed with spidery writing was at the bottom of the pile. With uncharacteristic enthusiasm Heimer picked it up, looked to see that no one was watching, and slipped it into his coat pocket. He would read this message later, in private.

Carter, his face as grim as ever, had been standing at the office door watching the street, through force of habit. Night was falling and the town's few shops were closing. Lamps were being lit and he was ready to take over the night shift at the office.

Heimer rose, put on his coat and announced that he was finished for the day. 'The place is all yours,' he told

Carter. 'You know where to find me if you need me.'

'We might all be needed,' the deputy said abruptly. 'There's three riders heading our way and by the look of their horses, they've been riding hard.'

Saunders joined his fellow deputy. 'I can see the two Hall kids but I don't know the man on the black horse.'

'I do,' Heimer told them quietly. 'His name's Wise and he's working for Sam Waldron. Sam reckons he's been hired to find a valuable horse that was lost around these parts but I don't believe that story for a minute. I reckon he's been out snooping around on the buffalo range.'

Carter looked at his boss in surprise. 'How do you know all that? I haven't seen him before.'

'I make it my business to know who's coming and going in this town.'

'I don't reckon it's right that some-one who ain't a real lawman should be sticking his nose into our work,' Saunders mumbled. 'We should be out checking on who's been raiding those buffalo camps and stealing hides.'

Carter was not so sure. 'We need to be a bit careful there. The town council hired us to look after the town. It ain't as if we were duly elected like county sheriffs and deputies. If we get mixed up in something outside the town limits, some smart lawyer could cut us to ribbons in a regular court.'

Saunders indicated the approaching riders. 'I reckon them three look like they're carrying bad news for us. We might get some action at last.'

'Don't be in such a hurry to get yourself killed,' Carter growled.

The riders halted before the sheriff's office and Notso dismounted, hitched his mare to the rail and went inside before the Halls.

'Is the sheriff here?' he asked.

'That's me, Fritz Heimer. What's troubling you, Mr Wise?'

Notso was a little surprised that Heimer knew him but quickly introduced himself and the two Halls, who were just entering the building. Then he set about describing the events of the last two days. The three lawmen listened in silence except that occasionally Heimer would interrupt to clarify some aspect of the narrative. When Notso paused for breath he asked Cyrus Hall, 'Do you agree with all that's been said?'

'Clair and I can only speak for what we saw today, but it happened like you just heard.'

Carter said suspiciously, 'How do you know that the men who pursued you were not after Wise here for some other reason? You only had his word that they were outlaws.'

'We had to take his word,' Clair explained. 'The risk of waiting to see if they had any good intentions was too big to take.'

'I agree,' Heimer told her. 'We know there's been trouble on the buffalo range. You did right.' He turned to Notso. 'I reckon these two young people should stay in town tonight and I'll get a statement from them in the morning. But I want you to sit down here and start writing. If there's been shooting I want to know all the details.'

Turning again to the Halls he asked, 'Do you folks have a place in town to stay?'

Cyrus nodded. 'We have a married aunt here, Mrs Doyle. I think she could put us up.'

'Good. Go now and get some grub and rest. See me here about ten in the morning.'

After the others had left Notso said that he needed to put away his horse.

'You stay right here. I'll get Gus to take your horse down to Tony Garcia's for the night and get it fixed up. When he gets back we can go for some grub and then start on that report. I'll let Sam Waldron know so he can be here too if he wants to be.'

'What happens now about those killers who wiped out Joe Long's camp and stole his hides? Every minute we talk here those wagons will be getting further away.'

The sheriff tugged at the end of his moustache and thought a while. Eventually he said, 'I ain't real sure there's a lot we can do tonight, but I'll figure out something by morning.'

Notso was hardly reassured by the doubting looks on the deputies' faces.

6

Sam had slept badly and was not in the best of moods when he and Notso met in his office the following morning. Hours of discussion in the sheriff's office had produced only mediocre results. Heimer was still unsure of legal jurisdiction but on a more certain note said that the town council would never agree to his raising a posse for which they had to pay. Unofficially, the sheriff agreed to send Gus Saunders to confirm Notso's claim that a crime had indeed been committed.

That decision did not please Notso. He pointed out that the deputy might not come back if he encountered the hide pirates. But Heimer assured them that the young deputy was no fool and would not blunder into dangerous situations.

Saunders greeted his new task with

enthusiasm. This was real work, he said, and was far more satisfying than keeping the town's few drunks in order.

Notso saw Saunders on his way to Sam's office as the deputy rode his pinto pony out of town. Later he told Sam, 'That deputy's taking a hell of a risk going out to Crooked Creek on his own.'

'At least it will stop him belly-aching. He was telling me on the quiet that he's fed up with the slow way Heimer is moving and wonders if he might not be in cahoots with the killers. I have been quietly getting to know Gus and he's already given me information that his boss would not like me to know. Maybe the ride out on the range will release a bit of his frustration, because he's keen to get after those murdering polecats.'

Notso leaned forward so he did not have to raise his voice. The less Florence knew of what was happening the better. He did not doubt her honesty but thought she might inadvertently reveal something while chatting with her friends.

'I reckon we're looking at this business from the wrong end, Sam. Nobody is going to steal hides unless they already have a market for them. When they are sold they have to be shipped away to Eastern tanneries. That gang is stopping people from following up their wagons when it would be smarter to head them off.'

'Don't you think I might have already thought of that? I've been studying maps and railroad schedules for the past week. The closest railroad station is about a hundred miles north-west of here at Cannon Flats. I reckon that's where they'll go. They might even be there by now.'

Notso disagreed. 'That place looks a bit too obvious. Where's the next station west of Cannon Flats?'

'There's a little whistle-stop called Monroe about twenty miles further on, but anyone trying to load hides there would attract attention. The next sizeable town is at Simpsons Creek and, going on the map, it could be another twenty-five or so miles.'

'So we're looking at about a hundred and fifty miles?'

'That's to go by train. Cross-country through Kelly's Gulch, it wouldn't be a hundred miles. What are you thinking?'

'If you can give me the right directions I could get there in fifteen hours easily. That is, if your clients will pay for another horse. Snowball has had a couple of days' hard riding and I don't want to break her down. The other horse does not need to be as good because I can nurse it along and it can be sold again when I get back.'

'I reckon another twenty or thirty dollars won't make a hell of a difference. But what do you do if you find the people you want? There are no brands on buffalo hides. How will you know them hide-pirates?'

'I'll sniff around a little and maybe buy a few drinks for some railroad people. If I think I am in the wrong town, I'll work back eastwards along the railroad line. Somebody will know something. I can send you a telegram if I find any names. The message will be 'so-an'-so sends regards'. You might have information on the name. I'll try to arrange another horse from Garcia and, if possible, get away today. Draw me a good map because I can't waste time following wrong trails.'

Garcia was happy to make another sale. The mount that Notso selected was a plain-looking black-legged bay. Though not eye-catching, he could find no real conformation faults when he checked it over. A test ride showed that the animal was sensible and well-broken. The forty-dollar price included a set of shoes, which Garcia would put on. He undertook to have the horse shod, fed and ready to travel by 2 p.m.

He was on his way back to Waldron's office when he met Clair Hall in the street. She looked nervous when she saw Notso and looked about her as he approached.

'Good morning, Mr Wise.' Suddenly she was very formal again.

Notso tipped his hat and replied equally formally. 'Howdy, Miss Hall. You are sounding mighty formal today. I hope I'm not in your bad books. There's an old rule in the rangers that folks who get shot at together are entitled to use first names.'

The girl smiled and her expression softened. 'I don't recall us being shot at.'

'We would have been if we had taken that trail over the hills, so I reckon the rule is flexible enough to include that. We've ridden a long way together, so that counts too.'

'I am sure you are inventing those rules, Notso, but I'll give you the benefit of the doubt. You are not in trouble with me even though we were business rivals for a while when we were looking for that horse. I'm sorry if I sounded unfriendly. It's just that today I am worried. I think I saw one of those men who were chasing us a few minutes ago on the street.'

'How would you know? They were

never close enough for us to see faces.'

'One was wearing a bright blue shirt and riding a roan horse. So was the man I saw this morning.'

Notso thought for a while. 'Roan horses are common enough among mustangs and a lot of folks around here ride mustang stock. And blue shirts are common, but it might be best if you tell Sheriff Heimer what you saw. Where did that rider go?'

'I don't know. He looked as though he was going to Garcia's livery stable but he must have turned off the street and gone down between the buildings. There are corrals behind some of them.'

'I'm going down that way to Waldron's. I'll have a bit of a look around. Meanwhile, tell the sheriff what you saw and if you see that man again, try to get a good description of him but don't draw attention to yourself. Where's Cyrus?'

'I left him at our aunt's place seeing to the horses. He will be along soon and we will be going to see the sheriff then. Do you have any suggestions about what I tell him?'

'Just say what happened. You have nothing to hide. Heimer has been around long enough to know that no two people see things exactly the same. It won't surprise him if your and Cyrus's accounts are different from mine. I'm sorry, but I have to go now. I have a busy day ahead. It's a job for Waldron. I hope we meet up again sometime soon.'

'So do I, and in accordance with that old ranger rule, please call me Clair.'

'That's a promise, Clair. Best of luck.'

As he walked away Notso's mind was racing. If Clair was right and one of their pursuers was in town, what was his purpose?

He walked down an alley that took him behind the buildings in the town's single street. As Clair had told him, there were several corrals and in one a roan horse was standing. There was no sign of a rider, who could have been in any of several nearby buildings. As Notso came closer he saw a shoulder brand of a capital S made into the form of a crooked arrow. It was not a brand he recognized.

Sam's office was not far away and Notso hurried there to bring his boss up to date on the latest developments.

7

Notso was travelling light, the bay horse unburdened with either rifle or saddle-bags. His only extra equipment was a small sack of oats. The horse had grown used to grain during its stay with Garcia and would not come down with gripes if it was fed the high-energy grain during a rest stop on the trail. Notso himself would eat when he reached his destination. His ranger experience had taught him that a hungry day or two would not kill him.

He left Woodville in the early afternoon, riding north-west with Waldron's map as a guide. His boss had been disturbed to know that Deputy Saunders had been allowed to venture alone into the dangerous buffalo range despite the latter's enthusiasm. The sheriff himself was showing little interest in the job and Deputy Carter was secretive and openly ambitious, keen to fill Heimer's boots when he retired. Waldron added that Saunders had occasionally supplied him with information and if he were killed the detective would lose a valuable insight into happenings with the local law.

Varying his horse's pace between walk, trot and lope, depending upon the ground, Notso made steady progress. The country gradually changed and the level grasslands gave way to rolling foothills by late afternoon. There were more trees on the slopes of sometimes steep, stony ridges, and after a sharp climb he would let the horse rest a while in the shade before continuing. Sam had told him that he needed to be in sight of Kelly's Gulch before the light failed, otherwise he might miss the trail.

He passed a couple of isolated cabins, and in a few more fertile spots there were homesteads in various stages of completion. He was tempted to stop and make enquiries, but he did not know what relationship the settlers might have had with the hide-pirates. Instead he called a friendly greeting or waved to people he encountered, but did not stop.

Counting his fingers held horizontally between the sun and the horizon, Notso figured that he had an hour of daylight when he suddenly sighted the notch in the blue line of hills ahead. He patted his horse's sweaty neck and said, 'There's Kelly's Gulch. Once we get there you can have a good feed and a decent rest for a while.'

They passed through the gulch just as night fell and a short time later came to the road that Sam's map showed leading to Simpsons Creek. At the first stream they encountered Notso dismounted and allowed the bay a good drink before riding off at a slower pace to find a resting spot. He found a place back from the trail sheltered by a stand of lodgepole pines. There he unsaddled the horse, rubbed its sweaty back and hung his saddle blanket on a bush to dry out a little. The horse was hungry and eagerly devoured the oats he had presented to it. Then he tethered it securely to a tree where it could rest. This done, he moved closer to the trail, finding a grassy spot on a slight bank that overlooked the road. There was no way of knowing whether the hide-pirates had already passed or were still to reach the spot, but he wanted to know if anyone came past in the night.

If any late traveller came along the trail later, Notso did not see or hear them because he had fallen asleep. He awoke a couple of hours later, cold, stiff and aching from the hard, damp ground. Moving briskly in the early morning chill, he saddled the horse and steered it down on to the trail.

The bay horse had recovered well from the previous day's long ride and seemed impatient with the steady pace to which its rider restricted it. Much as he would have liked to increase the speed, Notso did not want to risk an accident in the poor light.

Miles and hours slipped by and

suddenly it was light. Tracks of wagons and several horses showed on the trail but Notso saw nothing to indicate that they had been made by the hide-pirates. With good visibility he urged his mount to a canter, varied occasionally by a trot. Where the ground was rough underfoot he sometimes slowed to a walk, but the bay horse was a willing one, hardened by years of work on the cattle ranges and barring accidents, the rider knew it would reach Simpsons Creek by mid-morning.

Eventually they topped a rise and the town with its railroad track lay before them. Had it not been for the railroad, Simpsons Creek would not have existed, but it was a convenient place for the engines to take on wood and water. As he approached Notso weighed the advantages and disadvantages of the place. Its being a small cluster of houses and business premises would make it easier to search but the big disadvantage was that a stranger would be noticed immediately.

A long barnlike structure on the right side of the trail was the first building he encountered. The bare earth in front of it showed signs of wagon traffic and a couple of well-worn vehicles were parked outside. It would be a good place to start but he knew that he would need to have some answers ready to allay any suspicion. He was just riding towards the building when a man emerged from a side door, a hard-faced individual with a six-gun on his hip and an unfriendly look.

Notso said casually, 'Howdy. Is this a livery stable? I need somewhere to rest my horse for a while.'

'Ain't no stable here. This is a freight barn.'

'Is there somewhere in town where we can both eat and rest for a while?'

The suspicious one studied horse and rider. He saw a man travelling unprepared and a sweat-stained horse. He recalled that sometimes in his criminal past he had been in a similar situation. 'The Royal Hotel will put you up and it has a stall or maybe space in a corral for your horse — if you can pay.'

'I can pay.' Then, glancing about suspiciously, Notso asked, 'What's the law like around here?'

'Ain't none. There's a sheriff's deputy supposed to come around if there's trouble but mostly we fix it ourselves. Ain't seen him in months and nobody here is missin' the dumb sonofabitch.'

'That's good. Any work around here?'

'Depends what you're lookin' for.' The man's eyes strayed meaningfully to the gun on Notso's hip. It confirmed his impression that here was a man on the wrong side of the law.

'Who's likely to be hiring around here?'

'Big Jim Hardiman might give you a job on the buffalo range if you see him when he gets to town. He'll be along any day now.'

'I don't have a buffalo rifle and I sure as hell won't take on a lousy skinning job.'

'There could be other work but that's

up to Big Jim. If you're still around when he comes to town, see him.'

'Thanks for the help. I might do that.'

As Notso turned his horse to leave, he came close to an empty wagon, close enough to see white crystals of coarse salt on its floorboards; the type of salt that would escape from hides that had been salted and rolled for transporting. Then something else caught his eye. The wagon was muddy, especially around the wheels, but yellow paint was showing through the mud in places on a rear wheel. He knew then that this wagon had been in Long's camp at Crooked Creek. Carefully concealing any emotion he rode along the town's single street and quickly found the Royal Hotel.

The large, blonde lady at the desk looked as though she disapproved of the dishevelled newcomer, but he had the money and that was enough to get him a degree of respect and a room. She did not have to like the steady procession of such men who stayed a day or two and disappeared as quickly as they came. She reasoned, though, that any customers who paid their bills were better than having none at all.

Notso turned his horse over to the half-breed stableman and found the town's only restaurant. It was outside meal-times but reluctantly they served him a cup of muddy coffee and a slice of stale cake. That would have to suffice until the hotel dining room opened later. Then he found a barber shop where he was able to have a bath and a shave. Finally he went to the telegraph office and sent a message to Sam. They had worked out pre-arranged codes, where the most inno-cent messages had hidden meanings. In a few words his boss would know that the hides had been located and more developments were expected.

Notso did not know what gang mem-bers were already in town but he had a good idea of where to start looking for them.

The town's only saloon was easily identified by the row of horses hitched to the rail outside. The building was fairly new as it had only come with the railroad a few years before, but already its cheap paint was showing the effects of extreme heat and cold. Warped and splitting boards on the walls showed that the premises had been thrown together with green timber to supply the railroad construction workers. Business had fallen off since those days, but there were enough regular drinkers in the locality to keep the saloon going.

Notso pushed through the batwing doors and made his way to the bar. A couple of men who looked like cowhands were propped there, each with a drink in hand, an elbow on the bar and a foot on the brass rail. Another three men were trying their luck against a bored-looking gambler at a table in the back corner, but it was three men at a table near the door who caught his eye. They were types with which he was all too familiar. All appeared to be in their early thirties, wearing range clothes that had not seen too much hard work. They were lean, hard-looking, sporting holstered revolvers and full cartridge belts. All three had stopped talking and were eyeing him with an air of almost professional suspicion.

He pretended not to notice them, ordered a whiskey and passed a casual remark about the weather to the bartender.

The thin, elderly man behind the bar had seen the same approach a thousand times before. He agreed that the country looked good after the recent rain and waited for Notso to carry on the conversation, if he wanted to.

'Looks like things are pretty quiet around here.'

The barman nodded and said, 'We don't get many here in the middle of the day unless some ranchers are shipping cattle, but it's a bit early in the year for that. We get a few loads of buffalo hides shipped from here but not a lot of other stuff.'

'I would have thought this place was a bit too far from where most of the shooting is done. It seems a long way to cart hides.'

'It is a bit out of the way,' the thin man agreed, 'but Big Jim Hardiman has a warehouse here. He buys the hides from the buffalo camps, stores them until he has a couple of boxcar loads and then ships them East to tanneries. It's a good thing he does because his trade keeps the trains stopping here and occasionally someone starts a new business. Most towns on the railroad grow in time.'

Notso sipped his drink but found no reason to say more because at that moment a man came through the batwing doors. He was small, dark-skinned, wearing a red shirt and leaning on an improvised crutch. The leg of his trousers was split and a white bandage showed underneath.

One of the trio near the door called, 'Hey, Johnny, what did the doctor say about that leg?'

Creek Johnny replied, 'I'll live a hell of a lot longer than the coyote that shot me on Crooked Creek.'

8

Thoroughly alarmed, Notso did not turn but glanced in the mirror behind the bar. He immediately recognized one of the two men with whom he had swapped shots, but Creek Johnny was ignoring him and all his attention was centred upon his companions at the table.

Notso's luck was still holding. Without the distinctive black horse and with a shave and different clothes there was nothing to connect him with the man Creek Johnny had only seen fleetingly from a distance and mostly from the back. There was the white-handled gun, but such grips were common enough and he was not sure that his enemies had even noticed that small detail.

The injured man settled into a vacant chair and one of his companions walked to the bar to get another glass, because the whiskey bottle was already on the table.

He was small and fair-haired, with a straggling beard. With no attempt to hide his curiosity, he looked Notso up and down after the barman had given him the new glass. His opening comment sounded more like an accusation. 'I ain't seen you around here before.'

Notso sipped his drink and replied, 'That's probably because I ain't been around here before.'

'What brings you to these parts?'

Rather than object to this impolite questioning, Notso saw it as an opportunity to explain his presence. 'I'm heading for Montana but my horse is needing a rest so I reckoned I would give him a couple of easy days on good feed.'

'There's plenty of grass around at present,' the small man said suspiciously. 'Could it be that you left town in a hurry and have been travelling a bit too fast ever since?'

Notso had no trouble in sounding indignant. 'If I did, and I ain't saying I did, I reckon that's my business.'

The small man looked as if he was about to say something, but changed his mind and rejoined his companions. Through the reflection in the mirror Notso saw a few of the others glance in his direction as the curious one made some sort of remark that Notso heard only indistinctly. Then the small man sat down.

Now was not the time for a confrontation so Notso finished his drink and left.

At the telegraph office he found no reply to his telegram, so he sent another. Through a prearranged set of words he advised that he had some information. It read: *Put me on the list for Hannah's party.* The *list* meant that he had a name and the *party* referred to the hide thefts. The recipient of the telegram was shown as Florence Gower, Sam's secretary.

'I don't want to miss my sister's

birthday party,' Notso said, and hoped that he sounded convincing. The bored-looking telegraphist made no comment as he accepted payment and the completed telegram form.

Big Jim rode into town just as Notso was returning to his hotel. Though Notso had never seen him, it was easy to guess who he was despite his being roughly dressed and mounted upon a plain-looking horse. The three men riding with him looked more like bodyguards than companions as their restless eyes searched for possible trouble.

Big Jim glanced at the young man on the boardwalk and asked the rider beside him, 'Who's that?'

'Never saw him before,' Buck McDowell admitted. 'Could be the young fella who called at the freight shed today.'

'Find out. I want to know everything that goes on here.'

Big Jim had no doubts that he would soon know the stranger's name. He secretly had his henchmen competing with each other in reporting to him. Each thought he had been specially favoured and had been promised special rewards for his undivided loyalty. These men had no loyalty to each other, but would blindly follow their leader.

'Do you reckon he could be the law?' The speaker was a sharp-featured young man currently calling himself Andy Cooper. He was keen to demonstrate his skill with the pair of six-shooters hanging on his hips. 'I could fix him if you want.'

Big Jim was not so sure of Cooper's last claim but saw no reason to reprimand such eagerness. 'We don't want to spook him. Just let him go until we know exactly what he's up to. It strikes me he could be running from the law and might even prove useful to us. Pretend not to notice him but find out all you can. Half this town has been on my payroll at some time or other. Someone will know what this *hombre* is doing here. We'll have a couple of drinks and then I'll see the fella who runs the telegraph office. If our new friend has been sending messages I want to find out who he's writing to — and what he's writing about.'

Notso had a good meal at the hotel and turned in early that night, but as a precaution he propped a chair under the doorknob of his room and kept his Colt within easy reach.

The precautions were well justified because Big Jim had visited the telegraph office and a few not-too-subtle threats had quickly produced copies of the messages Notso had sent. At first glance they looked harmless enough, just a wandering rider checking with relatives about a birthday party for his sister, but the address in Woodville caught his attention. He had made a point of staying clear of that town because he did not have all the lawmen in his pocket. The less they saw of him the better. He noted the name of the addressee and returned to the saloon. A couple of his spies would check with his friends in town at regular intervals and he was sure one of them would know

Mrs Florence Gower.

He arrived back at the saloon in time to stop Andy Cooper from picking a fight with a big teamster. It would be a very one-sided affair if it came down to fists, but Cooper would be drawing a gun long before he got into that kind of trouble. His idea of a fair fight usually resulted in his opponent being shot.

Things were quiet in Simpsons Creek and Big Jim wanted them kept that way. It was foolish to attract the law's attention to the one place where he was relatively safe. 'Take it easy, Andy,' he warned. 'We want a nice quiet night.'

'The night will be quiet when I fix this big sonofabitch. It will only take a minute. I ain't scared of him.'

'That's good.'

Big Jim played another of his games. Of late Cooper had been getting too big for his boots. He walked up to where the pair were trading insults. 'If you want to fight both of you had better drop your guns. I'll make sure there's a fair fight and I'll shoot any man who

91

draws a weapon.'

Cooper went pale. This was not the one-sided gunfight he had planned. Too late he learned the folly of questioning his boss's orders. Any standing he had among his peers would be lost if he was to follow his instincts and try to weasel his way out of the trouble he had created for himself.

Tables and chairs were moved away and the drinkers in the bar quickly formed a ring. Big Jim told the pair, 'I'm the referee and the rules are that we won't waste time with round breaks. Just fight until one of you can't walk away. Now get at it.'

Cooper was younger and faster and charged in throwing punches from all angles. He had to stop the big man quickly before the latter could use his greater strength. Some of the blows landed but appeared to have little effect on the teamster. He almost casually ripped a left into the younger man's ribs and momentarily doubled him over, but then did not follow up his advantage, and he stepped back. A smile showed on his bearded face as he waited for Cooper to renew his attack. In the untidy scuffle that followed most of the attacker's punches fell on the big man's hands and forearms.

The teamster shuffled back almost awkwardly, but threw a straight left that caught the onrushing Cooper right in the mouth, mashing his lips against his teeth. Then, while his opponent was still in shock, he sent a right cross with the whole weight of his body behind it. The blow was perfectly timed and snapped the recipient's head to one side as he flew backwards and fell. No sooner had he hit the ground than the teamster reached down, grabbing the fallen man by his belt and shirtfront. He hauled him to his feet. With legs that would scarcely support him, Cooper was held upright.

'Do you reckon he can still stand?' the teamster asked Big Jim.

'Let him go and I'll see.'

Cooper's head was clearing but his

brain was still not functioning properly. He made the mistake of steadying himself and feebly raising his hands.

Big Jim wanted the lesson to sink in. 'I reckon he can go on for a while yet.'

The teamster swung a massive right hand and the impact was heard all over the bar. Cooper fell as though chopped off at the ankles. He would not be getting up in a hurry.

'You're the winner,' Big Jim told the teamster. 'Have a drink on me. None of my men will give you any trouble.' He looked at Cooper, who rolled over and was struggling to his feet with his face a mask of blood. 'I reckon now this young hothead has learned to take notice of what I tell him.'

The teamster had the free drink offered but left the bar shortly afterwards. He was uneasy in the presence of his new-found friends and there was an unmistakeable air of menace about them.

Buck McDowell, his eyes on the departing teamster, asked quietly, 'Do you want me to go after that jasper and put a slug in him?'

'Leave him be, Buck. Folks around here won't help us if they fear us, but if we show them a good side we can get all sorts of help from them. In six months' time when this fight has been forgotten, Cooper can bushwhack that teamster if he wants to and nobody will link it to us.'

'That big mule-skinner was a tough one. Cooper couldn't hurt him at all.'

Big Jim gave a grim but knowing smile. 'Being tough don't make him bullet-proof. Now let's relax for a while. We've had a busy time on the buffalo range.'

'What did you find out about that stranger?'

'His name's Wise,' Big Jim said. 'He was sending messages to someone in Woodville about a birthday party.'

'I know a few folks there, Jim. Who was he writing to?'

'Some woman called Florence Gower.'

McDowell's face took on an expression of distaste. 'I know her. She's a tough old biddy. Her husband got smart and died a couple of years ago. She worked in Ballard's store for a while but I heard later she got herself an office job somewhere.'

'What sort of office?' Big Jim asked suspiciously. 'I don't trust them people who work behind desks. They can be bigger crooks than we are.'

'I wouldn't have a clue who she works for, but Jimmy Hyland should be hitting town late tonight or early tomorrow morning. He spends a lot of time in Woodville. He'll know — if it's important — about where she works.'

'It could be. When Hyland gets in, ask him.'

9

Notso had a leisurely breakfast and stayed in his hotel room until he knew that the telegraph office would be open. The less he was seen, the better until he could develop a discreet line of enquiries.

The operator looked up as he entered the office. 'I just got another telegram for you. This must be some party your folks are planning. Telegrams are not cheap.'

Notso made no comment but took the message inside its special envelope, opened it and read. The message was brief but hardly comforting. It read: *Looking forward to seeing you,* which was a coded warning to cease operations and leave town as quickly as possible. Something was seriously wrong.

Trying to appear casual, he strolled back to the hotel and wasted no time settling his bill. His next visit was to the hotel stable where he knew that his horse had been fed and rested.

The groom was working on a roan horse when he arrived. The animal had been ridden hard and was being washed down. The brand on its shoulder was the crooked arrow that Clair had seen in Woodville.

'Looks like someone put a lot of miles under that one,' Notso remarked.

The groom replied, as he began scraping water from the animal's back with a piece of hoop iron, 'He's a mighty tough horse, this one. Belongs to a man named Hyland. He's Jim Hardiman's messenger boy. Just got in this morning from Woodville.'

'That's a fair ride,' Notso commented as he walked to the stall where his bay horse was waiting. His casual air concealed his satisfaction. He had another name and Hyland was Big Jim's link with someone in Woodville.

Not far away Hardiman was eating breakfast at a small kitchen attached to the freight barn. McDowell was with him. 'Hyland's up at the hotel,' the latter said. 'I was talking to him when he arrived. He had this for you.' McDowell passed over a sealed envelope.

Big Jim stopped eating long enough to stuff the envelope in a shirt pocket. He would read it later. 'Did you ask him about Florence Gower? I'm a bit suspicious of that name. I've heard it before somewhere.'

'You're right to be suspicious. Hyland says she works for a firm of private detectives. They have an office in Woodville. An *hombre* named Waldron runs it.'

Big Jim threw down his knife and fork and jumped to his feet, knocking over his chair as he did so. His face flushed with anger and a string of obscenities poured from his lips. But after a bit his rage cooled a little and he demanded, 'Why wasn't I told this earlier? Round up the boys and get that sonofabitch named Wise. He probably works for Waldron. Get him and get him quick. Who knows what he's found out already. Get moving!'

Within minutes McDowell was riding hard to start finding gang members who had spent the night in town. Some were sick with hangovers, others had slept late, but all shook off their lethargy when they knew that Big Jim was on the warpath.

Notso had just tightened his saddle cinches when he saw a couple of men running toward the stables, men he had last seen in the company of Big Jim. Conscious of the warning in the last telegram, he had no intention of waiting around. However, the new-comers were now blocking the exit from the corrals to the main street.

Any doubts as to their intentions were quickly dispelled when the pair began drawing their guns as soon as they saw him.

Knowing that men panting from running are not accurate pistol shots, Notso took a chance, swung aboard the bay and hit it with the spurs. His gun was in his hand before the horse had made two strides.

The gunmen skidded to a stop, raised their guns and separated in case they were run down. Both knew that a revolver bullet was unlikely to bring down a horse in full flight.

Notso fired at the nearer man, the one on his right. His shot struck home before the man had recovered from his surprise. The bullet staggered his target but the shooter had no time to see how successful his shot had been. The man on his left, still panting from his earlier exertion, was trying to peer through his sights for a properly aimed shot. A slug whizzed past Notso's head as the horse brought him close to the shooter, so close that he could see the alarm in the man's eyes. Leaning low in the saddle, he fired across his bridle hand. His target tried to jump away, tripped and fell backwards. Notso was unsure whether he had scored a hit but he was past the man and rapidly increasing the range when one of the pair fired at him, and again missed.

The bay horse burst from the lane between the buildings and wheeled on his hind legs as his rider steered him down the street.

Buck McDowell, mounted on a big grey horse, was barely fifty yards away, spurring towards the sound of the shooting.

Notso had the advantage of surprise and, in the seconds it took for the two horses to meet, he planted a shot in McDowell's chest at close range. The big man reeled in his saddle and dropped the gun he was cocking. By then Notso was past him but a backward glance showed his opponent tumbling from his saddle.

The shots brought men spilling from the doors of Big Jim's freight barn, but they were back from the road and none was carrying a rifle.

Hardiman was conspicuously present, yelling abuse as the man he wanted galloped past. Notso was uncertain as to whom the criminal boss was referring. It might have been him, or his own henchmen, or possibly both, but words could not hurt him.

Half a mile down the road Notso slowed his horse. It would be a long ride to Woodville and pursuit was certain. Survival would depend upon the staying power of his mount. He knew that his hunters would be pushing their mounts hard to catch up with him. He wanted the bay to be fully recovered from that first gallop when the pursuit came into view.

It had taken longer than expected to get Big Jim's men together and more time was lost saddling horses. Eventually Nate Masters took the trail with three men. Big Jim remained in Simpsons Creek to attend to the morning's casualties. He had one man wounded and McDowell, one of his most useful men, was dead.

Fred Ennis looked at his boss with a puzzled expression on his face. He felt he should have been riding with the others. But Big Jim had other ideas.

'Don't stand there like a tree full of owls, Fred. I have a special job for you. Get a wash and a shave and put on a coat. The train will be along in an hour and I want you in Monroe in case that Wise sonofabitch gives the boys the slip. If he ain't in town, see Ned Hayes. He'll give you a horse and a buffalo gun. Ride south and get that lawman as he goes through Kelly's Gulch. I want him dead.'

'But there's lawmen in Monroe, Big Jim. How will I get out again if I kill Wise there?'

'I picked you because, just between us, you're smarter than the others. Wait till there's no law or witnesses about. I have the Monroe lawmen in my pocket. They won't worry you and even if they have to arrest you for appearances' sake, you'll be allowed to escape. Now get moving. You have a train to catch. If Wise has gotten cunning and headed for the railroad, you'll see him at the station. If you're sure he ain't there, ride hard for Kelly's Gulch. You should get there before he does.'

* * *

Notso was surprised at the distance they had travelled before he saw his pursuers arriving. He had just finished reloading his gun when he first sighted a tiny dust cloud barely visible across the open prairie behind him. He urged his mount into a gallop for a short distance to create a dust cloud of his own and to attract attention. He figured that there was at least a mile between them and that Hardiman's men would have been riding hard to cut down the start he had gained. Now he wanted them to push their horses harder in an attempt to end the chase quickly. Then he slowed the bay horse to a fast trot.

Thinking that Notso may have been unaware of their presence or that his horse was failing, the hide-bandits liberally applied spurs and quirts in a final charge that they were sure would run down their quarry.

Riding steadily ahead, Notso glanced behind every few seconds and at last saw indistinct figures in the dust cloud that followed him. When the figures resolved into definite shapes of horses and riders, he reckoned it was time to go. He did not want to be shot down by someone dismounting and taking a carefully aimed shot with a buffalo rifle.

10

The bay gelding took off at a gallop as the rider nudged him with the spurs. He could hear the horses behind and sensed Notso's tension. The rider knew that the race would be won or lost in the next few minutes. Checking the animal's speed, he said quietly, 'Just slow down a bit, horse. I need them to think they might catch us. I want them to really hammer their horses before we try to shake them off.'

Nate Masters was pleased with the way his horse was overhauling the fugitive. The bay horse was either tiring or something was wrong with it. Yard by yard the hide-pirate's mount was gaining on the horse ahead. It was also lengthening the gap between itself and the other pursuers. In a bid to end the chase quickly, Masters was gambling that his horse had the speed and stamina to overhaul their quarry before the chase went too far.

Notso glanced over his shoulder. The rider on the large bay horse was within fifty yards of him and would soon be in dangerous pistol range. He had a lead of about a hundred yards on the other three. Gradually a plan was forming in Notso's mind. It would require split-second timing and he had to find the right place but until then he could only hope that his horse could keep on its feet and that he was not the victim of a lucky shot.

Half a mile later Notso found the place he sought. The trail crossed a low but steep ridge; a rider ascending it could not see what was on the other side until he came on to the crest. In the fraction of a second available, the pursuer would have no chance of stopping his horse.

Steadying the bay slightly, Notso checked it after it crossed the ridge, spun it in a half-circle and drew his gun. He was just in time.

Masters came pounding over the ridge and suddenly found that he had caught the one he was chasing. The problem was that Notso was waiting for him squinting down the barrel of his .45. It was all totally unexpected and the hide-pirate had no time to explore the few options he might have had. Instinctively he hauled back on the reins as he clawed for his gun, but the thrill of the chase was on the horse and it could not stop quickly. To its rider's horror, it sat back on its haunches, but the momentum slid it forward on the hard-baked clay of the trail.

Masters was almost at the muzzle of Notso's gun, and despairing of bringing his own weapon into action, he frantically threw himself sideways: anything to escape that deadly black bore confronting him. He was too late; a bullet took him in the chest and sent him rolling in the dust in an untidy tangle of arms and legs.

Notso spun the bay horse again and it shot down the slope just as the other riders topped the crest.

They saw Masters covered in blood and dust trying feebly to move, his riderless horse and Notso spurring away. Suddenly the trio lost all enthusiasm for their task.

'I've gotta help Nate,' Roy said.

Another said, with some justification, 'My horse is done. It ain't gonna catch that other one.'

Andy Cooper agreed. 'Even if my horse was good enough, which it ain't, there's no way I'd go after that sonofabitch on my own. Let's just tell Big Jim that his horse was too good.'

'How do we explain what happened to Nate?'

'Simple. His horse was good enough but he wasn't. Is he still alive?'

'Don't look like it,' Roy said as he leaned from his saddle to view the fallen man. 'There's blood everywhere and no one can lose that much and still be alive. I suppose we better get him across his saddle and take him back. Big Jim won't be happy.'

A mile away, Notso slowed his horse to a walk. Hardiman's men had given up the chase. Now he had to nurse his mount along, for there were still many miles to travel.

★   ★   ★

Fred Ennis left the train at Monroe and saw that no one had boarded it. He felt a certain relief that he was no longer expected to shoot his man in such a public place, but he did not relish the long ride to Kelly's Gulch.

Half an hour later he rode out of town on a horse that Ned Hayes had supplied, with a Sharps rifle across his saddle and a pocketful of big cartridges. He made one stop along the way and fired a couple of test shots at improvised targets just to ensure that the sight settings were accurate. Satisfied that they were, he climbed back on his horse and pointed it south. If all went well he would reach the gulch in daylight ahead of Notso. The big bullets in his pocket would inflict serious damage and a more sensitive man might have pitied any person on the receiving end of one. To Ennis another death meant nothing.

* * *

Clair was trying to persuade Florence to let her see Waldron but the secretary kept insisting that he was too busy to see her. Sam heard the raised voices and decided to intervene. 'It's all right, Florence,' he called. 'I can see Miss Hall for a few minutes.'

Ignoring Florence's icy glare, Clair walked through the open office door. 'Thank you for seeing me, Mr Waldron. I won't take up too much of your time.'

Sam remained seated but indicated a chair. 'Excuse me not getting up but this leg is still troubling me. Take a seat and tell me what the problem is.'

Clair sat down, thanked him and broached the subject of the reward he had advertised for the missing stallion.

'My brother and I were hoping to find that horse. Is the reward still on offer?'

Sam thought fast. 'I'm afraid it's not,' he said. 'The matter is closed.'

'I saw your man, Wise, leaving town and thought he might have gone after it.'

'Notso's on another job for me but I would prefer not to discuss it.'

'I like to mind my own business, Mr Waldron, but I have a suspicion that the work he's on might have something to do with those men who tried to waylay us the other day. I think I saw one of them in town. I recognized the horse he was riding.'

Sam stroked his moustache, leaned closer and asked quietly, 'Have you told the sheriff about this? I think it would interest him.'

'I'm a bit wary of going near the sheriff's office because the man I saw was talking to someone through a side window there. I'm not sure whom I can trust.'

'Why are you telling me this?'

Clair said sharply, 'Because Notso works for you and I'm sure he hasn't come out here looking for lost horses. Talk around town is that you are investigating the murders and robberies on the buffalo range. If those stories are right, it means that people no longer trust our local lawmen, and from what I saw, they have good reason.'

Waldron raised a hand as if to steady the rush of words. 'Don't be too quick to judge,' he warned. 'Sheriff Heimer has a jurisdictional problem and has to tread carefully.'

'You make that problem sound like a medical complaint,' Clair accused. 'I thought I would warn you that something was wrong with our local lawmen, but it seems that you don't want to know.'

'I assure you, Miss Hall, that I do want to know what's happening but I won't condemn a good peace officer on the grounds of local gossip. You are right, Notso is investigating what has been happening on the buffalo range. The missing horse story was to justify his presence in the area, but the cat is out of the bag now. I am sorry that I misled you and your brother but it was for my man's safety. Please don't tell anyone about this. It will put Notso in even greater danger than he is already.'

'He's in danger?'

Waldron looked grave. 'He is. I don't want you to get the wrong impression. I am very grateful for the information you have given me, but I must be careful how I use it. Rest assured that what you told me will not be ignored. Things are not what they seem here in Woodville and your discretion is vital. Are you staying in town?'

'Yes. My brother has gone back to our homestead but I have decided to have a while with my aunt. It's nice to have another woman to talk to sometimes. The prairie can be a lonely place.'

'Sometimes it's better to be lonely than be at risk from other people. Be very careful, Miss Hall.'

11

The sun was setting in a blaze of red and gold when Notso halted the bay beside a small stream. There was an abundant growth of buffalo grass and it was a good place to rest his mount. He was satisfied that nobody was on his trail. He unsaddled the horse, rubbed its back, and when it had cooled down he led it to the creek for a drink. Then he allowed it to graze on the end of his lariat while he stretched out and rested. He was not far from Kelly's Gulch and still had a long way to ride, but another hour would not make a great deal of difference. It was easier to keep his mount fresh than to kick along a tired horse, and moving at a better pace would make up some of the lost time.

It was fully dark when he gave the horse another drink and saddled it. There would be no more water until they reached Woodville. The night would be a moonless one and he would have to be careful that, once through the gulch, he did not stray off the trail. Stepping into the stirrup, he swung himself into the saddle and patted the horse's neck. 'Time to get going, partner. The sooner we reach Woodville the better.'

* * *

Ennis was getting worried. He was sure that Notso would have reached the gulch in daylight and was surprised when he did not. There was always the possibility that Big Jim's other men might have ridden him down, and after a couple of hours sitting in darkness he had almost convinced himself that such was the case. Then he heard a horse approaching. Quickly he grabbed the big rifle, rested it in the fork of the stunted cedar that concealed him and sighted it on the trail fifty yards away. Then the shot that would have been simple in daylight was suddenly found to be difficult. In the poor light he could not see his rifle sights properly.

The horse was moving at a fast walk, just an indistinct blur in the gloom. With little time to waste, Ennis took another cartridge from his pocket and held it between the fingers of his left hand in case a quick follow-up shot was needed. Then he drew back the big side-hammer and tried to line up his target. A vague shape moved into his field of vision.

Notso was quite sure that he had shaken off the hunters and was simply concentrating on getting home. Some-where off to his right a twig cracked and automatically he looked towards the sound. A red streak stabbed at him from the rising ground and the roar of a big rifle boomed like thunder in the walls of the narrow gulch.

His horse gave a startled jump and spun in a circle, almost unloading its rider. In panic the animal circled again while Notso fought to control it.

Ennis moved like lightning, flipping down the trigger guard and ejecting the spent shell. He had a second cartridge in the breech and managed to get off another shot as his target fled back the way he had come. But as the shots were still echoing he heard a cry of pain.

Notso was on the ground, rolling away into the shadows of the bushes beside the trail. The bay horse tried to move off but stood on the dropped reins and remained, snorting nervously, a few yards away. Two shots with the one rifle from the same place told him that there was only one shooter and now Notso set a trap of his own. He broke a few twigs, gave what he hoped sounded like a moan of pain and quietly crawled back through the shadows toward the ambush spot.

Ennis was a relieved man. Missing with the first shot, he considered himself lucky that the second shot had found its target. The nervous snorting of the victim's horse a short distance down the trail was a sure sign that the man had not fled out of range. The groans and crackling brush indicated that he had been hit badly. But the shooter was no fool who would rush out to see the results of his marksmanship. He remained where he was and smoked a cigarette. It was better to let the man die of his wound before venturing too close.

The flaring match as Ennis lit up and the tiny red glow of the cigarette told Notso what he needed to know. Carefully he edged closer, drew his gun and waited.

After what seemed like hours but was only minutes, the crackling of brush announced that the shooter was coming to investigate. Ennis drew reassurance from the nervous snuffling of the riderless horse. Any normal man would have ridden to safety, so he was sure that Notso was dead or close to it. Nevertheless he had reloaded the rifle and held it ready for use. Reaching the trail, he saw the dim shape of the horse and expected to find the rider nearby. But the rider was closer than he realized.

Notso came out of the shadows right

beside him, left hand grabbing the rifle barrel and right hand slamming a six-shooter against Ennis's temple.

The surprised man dropped to his knees, losing his grip on the rifle as he did so. Another hit with a gun barrel stretched him on the ground. Almost unconscious, he heard a hard voice cutting through the waves of pain he felt in his head.

'Make one wrong move and you're dead.'

With warm blood trickling down his face from a gashed scalp, Ennis gasped urgently. 'Don't shoot. I won't do anything.'

'That's nice to know. Very carefully now, unbuckle that gunbelt. You have a cocked gun against your head, so no tricks.'

'Be careful,' Ennis pleaded. 'That gun could go off.'

'I can't say a murdering skunk like you would be any loss if it did, so what if you be careful for the two of us?' Notso picked up the man's revolver and tucked it in his belt. 'Now I'll have the rest of your artillery. Your type usually has a hideout gun or a knife somewhere.'

'There's a derringer in my inside coat pocket.'

'Get it out very carefully and throw it away. Anything else?'

'There's a knife in my boot top.'

'You know what to do with it. I intend to search you and will shoot you right here if I find any other weapon.'

Ennis threw the knife after the derringer. 'That's all, I swear.'

Having satisfied himself as to the veracity of that statement, Notso picked up the rifle. 'You didn't walk out here. Let's get your horse. We can talk on the road to Woodville.'

'You can take me anywhere you like but you won't make any charges stick. I'll deny everything. It will be your word against mine. I know I'll have a good lawyer.'

'You might need an undertaker before you need a lawyer. You don't play by the rules and neither do I. There won't be too much argument if I bring you in dead. Chances are that some lawman is already looking for you. Now let's get our horses.'

Half an hour later the pair were riding to Woodville. Ennis had both hands tied to the saddle horn, and a lariat with a noose around his neck, the other end fastened to the horn of Notso's saddle. His captor held the reins of the prisoner's mount. Should he attempt to escape or if the horse took off for any reason, Ennis was a dead man. Consequently, he sat very nervously and quietly on his horse. In response to questions, though, he was surly and defiant. He claimed that his name was John Smith and that in the dark he had mistaken Notso and his horse for a buffalo. Though aware that his unlikely story was totally disbelieved, the captive would maintain it until he reached Woodville, where several people knew him. By then he would have the services of a lawyer and Big Jim would be doing his utmost to secure his release.

Hardiman's face went white with suppressed anger when his hunters returned to his barn with the wrong corpse across the saddle of a led horse. His first impulse was to scream abuse at his incompetent henchmen, but with a rapidly deteriorating situation he decided that it was best not alienate them. He needed every man he could exploit. While seething inside he tried outwardly to appear philosophical. 'That's bad luck,' he said quietly. 'But there's still a good chance that Ennis will get him as he goes through Kelly's Gulch. He has orders to ride straight back to Monroe and send a telegram when the job is done. We should hear tomorrow morning at the latest.'

'What happens if he misses him?' asked the skinny one, Isaac, the most vocal of his men.

Big Jim was unsure of what to do in such an event, but had to pretend that he had explored all possibilities. 'I've thought of that already. Chances are that if Ennis failed he's dead, so them sneaking detectives won't learn anything from him.'

The questioner was not satisfied and put up another hypothetical question. 'Suppose something goes real wrong and Ennis gets hisself captured?'

That possibility also worried Big Jim but he was not prepared to discuss his fears at this stage. 'We have the law in our pocket,' he told them with a confidence he did not feel. 'Ennis knows enough to keep his mouth shut. I can get him a good lawyer who can soon figure out how serious the case against him is. If it looks weak, we can fight it in court but if it looks bad, we can bust him out of jail. Now, you fellas get a bit of rest. In the morning I might need you in a hurry.'

As his men sauntered away, Roy said to the others, 'Big Jim should be called 'Tarpaulin' on account of the way he gets everything covered.'

Hardiman heard the remark and

fervently wished it was true. Notso had caused him more worry than any lawman to date. His run needed to be brought to an end as quickly as possible.

12

Notso and his prisoner arrived at the Woodville sheriff's office before Heimer reported for work. Jack Carter was already there and his sour face reflected his disapproval of this unexpected problem. 'What's going on here, Wise?' he demanded.

'My friend here had a good try at ambushing me last night at Kelly's Gulch. I'm sure he's connected with the gang that wiped out Joe Long's camp. I want him held in jail.'

'On what charge?'

'Attempted murder will do for a start and I'm sure that if we dig around there will be a few other misdeeds in his past.'

Carter turned to the prisoner. 'What do you say to all this?'

'I'll say plenty when I get a lawyer. I was just minding my own business when this crazy coyote jumped me last night. I ain't done nothin' and I sure as hell ain't sayin' nothin' until I get a lawyer.'

Sheriff Heimer's arrival saved Carter from making a difficult decision. 'I'll take over now, Jack,' he said to the deputy. 'Let's get this man off his horse and into a cell.'

'Are you sure that's right, Sheriff? There's only one man's word for what happened. The prisoner denies the whole thing. If it happened at all, it happened at Kelly's Gulch, which is way out of our territory.'

'We can worry about that later. I'm putting this man in a cell.' Heimer stopped and fixed his gaze on Notso. 'I'll hold him this morning but if you and Sam Waldron don't have something serious against him by tonight, I'm turning him loose.'

Notso wasted no time in getting back to Sam's office and reporting what he had learned. His boss was glad to see him as he had been worried that he might have stayed too long in Simpsons Creek. Though it was too late to stop the shipment of stolen hides he now had the name of the gang leader and knew where the stolen hides had been stored. A little more detective work would quickly disclose the Eastern destination of the hides.

'How did you know to warn me about getting out of Simpsons Creek?' Notso asked.

Sam gave a tight little smile. 'You're not the only one I have working for me but I have to keep some secrets. Let's say that my informant saw how things were building up and warned me. In turn, I warned you. Big Jim Hardiman and his crew are not as smart as they think. That yellow wagon wheel you reported ties him to the attack on Long's camp, and I have the serial numbers of three Sharps buffalo rifles that were delivered through this office to Long just before his last trip. I was acting as agent for the hide contractors. They were stolen along with the hides and, unlike hides, they can be identified. If they turn up somewhere they shouldn't, someone will be in a heap of trouble.'

Notso suddenly remembered. He exclaimed, 'The rifle that skunk tried to shoot me with was a Sharps .50, just about brand new. It might be worth checking it against your list.'

Sam struggled to his feet and reached for his crutches. 'You could be right. I'll bring that receipt along. We're going to see Heimer.'

The sheriff showed uncharacteristic eagerness as he produced the rifle lately taken from the prisoner and passed it to Sam. 'If those numbers match, we might start getting somewhere at last.'

'The number matches. It's the second one on the list.' Passing rifle and receipt back to Heimer, the detective told him, 'We have this sonofabitch facing murder charges now. Don't think of letting him go. This rifle ties him to the attack on Long's camp. Now let's start asking a few questions.'

The questioning was only partially successful. Ennis gave his true name, but denied any wrongdoing and despite threats and appeals to his non-existent better nature, refused to divulge anything else until a lawyer was present.

Notso wrote out a statement, which he copied before leaving the signed original with the sheriff. He was hungry, tired and looking forward to a few hours of uninterrupted sleep. As he made his way toward Reed's hotel he met Gus Saunders, who was about to commence the night shift at Heimer's office.

'Howdy, Notso,' the deputy greeted cheerfully. 'I heard you brought in a prisoner today.'

'That's right. I think you will have the dubious pleasure of his company for quite a while. He might need a lot of watching.'

'Jack and I will watch him,' the deputy chuckled. 'Old Fritz is the one most likely to do something careless if he's left alone. The job is getting beyond him and his heart is not in it these days.'

'I've seen that breed of skunk before,' Notso said seriously. 'Our friend Ennis strikes me as a mighty dangerous character. Don't take any chances with him.'

'I can handle him and I'm telling you now that the law will be saved the cost of a trial if he tries any monkey business on me. One thing I have learned about being a lawman is that you make a lot of your own luck, so I am always careful around prisoners.'

'That's a good idea. You live a hell of a lot longer that way.'

'Things are going to be different around here when Heimer retires. He's let things slide too much and Jack and I both agree that the law around here will be a lot better when he gets out of the way. In theory the two of us are in the running for his job, but there's always the chance that the town council might bring in some outsider with a big reputation. If that happens I might see Sam Waldron about a job. Do you think he might have a vacancy?'

'I don't know,' Notso confessed. 'I'm only new there myself but the idea might be worth a try. Meanwhile be very careful around Ennis.'

'I'm running a bit late, so I have to go, but you're worrying too much, Notso. I can look after myself.'

'I sure hope you can,' Notso muttered — to himself, for the deputy had already walked briskly away, eager to begin work. Notso still had some doubts. Excessive confidence when dealing with desperate men had killed more than one lawman.

He ate well and turned in early. Despite the rattle of wagons and voices in the nearby street, he quickly fell asleep.

Next morning, rested, fed and suitably cleaned up, he loitered a while in the street. It was too early in the day for Waldron and Heimer and he was idly looking in the window of a saddler's shop when he saw Clair walking towards him. She smiled when she saw him and he felt a strange sense of elation, as though he was meeting someone special to him.

You hardly know her, he silently told

himself as he returned the smile and tipped his hat in greeting. 'A nice morning for a walk,' he ventured.

'It certainly is. I didn't expect to see you back in town. Mr Waldron thought you would be away for a while.'

'This job is a bit unpredictable and the telegraph doesn't help. It makes things too easy for people like Sam to switch a fella all over the countryside. It was a lot easier when orders were carried by hand or even sent through the mail.'

Clair laughed. 'I agree with you there, Notso. Telegrams are expensive but a lot of folks are using them now. The last few days there have been a few rough-looking types hanging around the telegraph office. I passed it just a while ago and one was yelling at the operator because he was expecting a message that had not come through.'

'I thought you would have been back at your homestead,' he told her.

'I'm going in the next couple of days. I can't stay away too long. Cyrus gets the place in a mess and doesn't eat properly if he's left alone for any length if time.'

'Do you live far from town?'

'We are eight miles out, only about two hours' easy ride.'

'Let me know when you are going and I'll escort you home. There are some mighty bad *hombres* roaming around at present.'

'That's very nice of you,' Clair said. 'But I'm sure no one will bother me.'

Notso contradicted her. 'Don't be too sure. You and Cyrus could be in trouble if those characters that tried to ambush us think you might have recognized them. Don't try going home on your own. If I am away, see Sam and he might arrange with Heimer for a deputy to escort you.'

'I don't think I would like that idea. Jack Carter is so serious that his face would break if he smiled, and Gus Saunders reminds me of a big, enthusiastic dog bounding around the place and getting under foot in his efforts to be helpful. But I'm not sure I could trust any of our local lawmen.'

'Why's that?'

'I saw the man who rides that roan horse talking to someone through the side window of Heimer's office, but I couldn't see who he was talking to. Didn't Sam Waldron tell you? I told him because I didn't know who else to tell.'

'There's been a few things happening and it probably slipped Sam's mind. I'll check with him about it, but don't think of going home on your own.'

'I think you are worrying too much. I'm no threat to these people.'

Notso frowned and said in a serious tone, 'They don't know what you saw or didn't see but people like them don't take chances with any stray witnesses. I have to see Sam now but promise me you won't try to go home alone.'

Clair laughed. 'I promise. Anything to make you happy.'

As he walked on Notso became aware that her promise had made him happier than he'd expected. Silently he reproached himself. *Don't get too many big ideas.*

Florence was gradually getting used to Notso and now waved him through to Sam's office without the usual attempt at interrogation. Unbidden, he seated himself in the visitors' chair and for the next few minutes the pair discussed the most recent aspects of the case. They now had a few names: Big Jim, Ennis and the messenger, Hyland. Progress had been slow but Notso's trip to Simpsons Creek had yielded a considerable amount of new information.

Notso mentioned the hardcases that Clair had seen hanging about the telegraph office, but it seemed that Sam already knew about them.

'That's to be expected,' the detective said. 'Messages will be flying back and forward. Hardiman will be organizing a lawyer for Ennis and trying to plan his next move.'

'Is there some way we can round up some of those characters hanging about the telegraph office?'

'It's best we leave them as they are for a while. We don't want to tread on Fritz's toes and, though they don't know it, those ugly sonsofbitches are making my job easier.'

Notso was about to ask how when the sound of gunfire erupted.

'Get down there quick,' Sam ordered. 'That's coming from the sheriff's office.'

13

Notso reached the sheriff's office at the same time as Heimer himself arrived. Panting from the unaccustomed exercise, the lawman launched himself through the door with a drawn gun.

Notso was a couple of yards behind him and dreaded hearing a renewed burst of shooting but it did not happen. He followed Heimer through the dividing door that separated the cells from the office. Gun smoke and the smell of burnt powder still hung in the air.

Gus Saunders still held a gun in his hand and he was pointing to the form of Ennis, who was crumpled against the cell bars. 'He had a gun. He had two shots at me. The gun's there on the floor of the cell. I had to shoot him.'

Heimer glanced at the dead man and then at his deputy. 'Are you hit, Gus?'

'He missed me. I think he was

hampered by trying to shoot between the cell bars. Where did he get the gun?'

Notso looked at the weapon on the floor. It was a Navy Colt with a cutdown barrel that had been converted to fire metallic .38 cartridges. 'Looks like a hideout gun, but I can tell you now, he didn't have it when I handed him over to you people.'

The sheriff nodded. 'I can vouch for that. He didn't have any gun on him when we put him in the cell. I searched him myself. Did anyone come to see him?'

'Not while I've been here. Jack was on guard through the night. He didn't mention any visitors when he went home this morning.'

Heimer looked angry. Turning to Saunders he growled, 'Get round to Carter's and bring him back here. I want to hear what he has to say about all this.'

Notso saw that he was not needed and said, 'If you don't need me, I'll get back to Sam. He's pretty clumsy with those crutches and is likely to break his other leg trying to get here.'

Heimer remained deep in thought and only muttered, 'Suit yourself.'

Sure enough, the detective was struggling along on his crutches when Notso met him on his way back. 'What's happened?' he demanded.

Notso told him as they retraced their steps to his office. To his surprise the detective took the news quite calmly.

'There's something not right in Fritz's office and I've been expecting a deal like this. Someone was frightened that Ennis would talk and I reckon at least one of our lawmen has something to hide. That young Saunders fella has been quietly complaining to me for a while. He reckons the sheriff ought to be doing a lot more than he is about those hide-pirates, says he spends a lot of time writing letters and that's a fact. I know that he also gets a lot of letters from Simpsons Creek.'

'How do you know that?'

'Some years ago, in my ranger days, I

141

let a small-time rustler go. He had only rustled a couple of calves from a much bigger rustler and I reckon I scared him back on to the straight and narrow.'

Notso was amazed. 'You let a rustler go? You had a reputation for being the scourge of rustlers. You were supposed to be the meanest critter north of the Rio Grande. Everyone said you were hell on rustlers.'

'There's rustlers and rustlers and I was a bit lenient sometimes on poor folks who were stealing to feed their families from wealthy men who themselves were rustlers on a large scale. But, as I was saying, that reformed rustler is now running the post office here and owes me a favour. He won't allow tampering with the mail but has noticed a lot of letters coming and going between Fritz and a certain Mr Wilson at Simpsons Creek. Things were looking fishy before today but now they look downright bad. Young Saunders is very idealistic and not very discreet. Occasionally he has expressed doubts to me about his boss. If the gang has a deal with Heimer, that could be why Ennis tried a jail break today. The other possibility is that someone needed to shut Ennis up. Someone might reckon it was safer to have him dead rather being free and likely to be recaptured.'

'If that's the case, who gave the order?'

'That's what we have to find out. I'll start asking around. It's surprising the amount of information picked up from people who don't realize that they have it.'

'I'm not sure I'm cut out for this detective stuff, Sam. Life was a lot simpler when someone just shot at you and you shot back.'

'You'll get used to it. Meanwhile we should be figuring out how Ennis got that gun. He didn't find it in the cell. Did Carter or Heimer give it to him or did Saunders shoot him and toss the gun into the cell after he fired a couple of shots? I heard about four shots but could not tell how many guns were involved. There's another possibility too. Supposing Saunders gave Ennis the gun, they disagreed about something and both started shooting.'

Notso thought for a second or two. 'That's a possibility, but I have the feeling that he would let him out of the cell before he gave him the gun.'

They returned to Sam's office and between them explored all possible angles of the situation. Sam had amassed a considerable amount of information but much of it did not fit the picture that was emerging.

'Big Jim's pretty smart,' Sam admitted. 'He seems to have people everywhere, who keep him informed about every move the law makes. I know for a fact that he has a couple of Western Union telegraphists in his pocket and he has regular couriers running between towns with messages. As well as that, if Clair Hall is right, he has a contact in the sheriff's office. We have to face the possibility that maybe all of our law officers here are crooked.'

Notso was surprised. 'All three of them?'

'Until we know better we don't rule anyone in or out. Fritz Heimer is a lot smarter than most folks think and who knows what Jack Carter thinks. He don't say much to anyone. I don't think Saunders is smart enough for the dirty work that's going on around here. He might follow but I'm pretty sure he's not a leader.'

'Why don't we stop trying to be too clever and just haul in Big Jim?'

Waldron shook his head. 'We can't do that. There's not enough to hold him on.'

At this point Florence came to the office door wearing her usual disapproving look. 'Mr Waldron, Miss Hall is here. She wants to see you. Should I ask her to wait?'

'No. I'll see her now. Send her in.'

Clair came through the door and Notso jumped up to get a spare chair for her. 'I'll go if you want to talk in private,' he volunteered.

'That won't be necessary. You might both want to hear what I have to say,' Clair told him. 'I saw that man who rides the roan horse just a while ago. He was on foot but I am sure it was the same man.'

'The one you think could be part of the gang?' Sam prompted.

'That's right. He was coming out of the Western Union office.'

'Could be he's been reporting the Ennis killing to Big Jim,' Notso suggested. 'Do you think we could hold him somehow?'

'On what charge?' Sam challenged. 'We have to turn him over to the local law and I have a feeling that they would let him go.'

'What does he look like?' Notso asked.

'He is about thirty, average height, but skinny build. He's wearing a blue-and-white striped shirt, a black leather vest, brown pants and a light-brown hat with a high crown. He has one gun with a wooden handle worn on the left side with the butt facing forward.'

'That's a mighty good description,' Sam said. 'You are a very observant young lady.'

'Thank you. Would you like me to follow him and see who he talks to?'

'That might not be a good idea,' Notso suggested. 'He's sure to notice a pretty girl like you trailing along behind him. I'm sure I would.'

'He's right,' Sam told her. 'With your description Notso should be able to pick him up, and he can look mighty ordinary when he wants to. He's had a bit of practice at this sort of thing. Wait here until Notso leaves the office so you are not seen together. I might be able to throw a bit of work your way if you are interested.'

Clair and Sam were deep in conversation when Notso made his way onto the street. He looked about but saw no one on the street matching the suspect's description, so he made his way to Garcia's livery stable. While pretending to check on his two horses he looked around for the roan horse, but did not see it. He was not surprised. Given the number of miles Big Jim's man was riding, it was logical that he would change mounts.

Garcia was grooming a seal-brown gelding that Notso had not seen at the stable before. He went straight to the point. 'Howdy, Tony. Who owns that horse?'

Between brush strokes Garcia replied, 'He belongs to a man named Jim Hyland. Mostly he rides a roan horse but lately it's had a lot of work so he's changed to this one.'

'What does Hyland do? He must come here often. I remember seeing the roan horse. Seems this *hombre* is a good judge of horses.'

'I do not know what he does and I do not ask. As long as he does not try to harm me I will mind my own business.'

'Do you reckon he might be dangerous?'

The liveryman shrugged. 'He has a hard look about him and any man carrying a gun can be dangerous. I would not take risks with a man like that.'

'That's sure good to know,' Notso said, 'because he is just coming around the corner of the barn.'

14

Hyland's eyes narrowed as he saw Notso standing near his horse talking to Garcia. Momentarily he hesitated, but then, with the confidence of someone protected, he walked aggressively up to the other pair. 'What are you doing with my horse?' he demanded.

Notso replied, 'Tony's grooming him for you and I'm talking to Tony. You can relax; he's being well cared for. What happened to your roan horse? Did you wear a couple of inches off its legs carrying messages for Jim Hardiman?'

Surprise showed briefly on Hyland's face. He had not expected to be recognized although he was aware of Notso's identity. 'Mind your own business, Wise,' he snarled. 'You ain't a proper lawman and I don't have to tell you anything.'

'You are my business and you have

already told me more than you intended. Your friend in the sheriff's office won't be able to help you, and if you land in a cell Big Jim is likely to have you killed the same as he did Ennis.'

'I don't know what you're talking about, so just shut your face. I ain't busted no laws around here.'

'You might be right but if we hold you for a while and send a few telegraph enquiries about your background, I am sure that more than one lawman would be keen to talk to you.'

Hyland's hand strayed closer to his gun butt. 'Are you going to try taking me in?'

'Not at this stage. I want you to go back and tell that skunk in Simpsons Creek that we know what he's been up to and soon expect to have him and all his friends behind bars. If you have half a brain, you will then get on your horse and keep moving. When we get Hardiman, all those with him will go too.'

Notso was bluffing when he made

that statement but knew that Hyland would relay it to his boss. He wanted to worry Big Jim into making a premature move. Left unhindered to plan his moves, Hardiman had stayed one jump ahead of those who would seek to have him charged with any infraction of the law.

Ignoring Notso, the messenger ordered Garcia, 'Look after that horse well. I might be here for a couple of days but I want it well fed and ready to travel — and keep your mouth shut about my business.'

Having done what he set out to do, Notso left the pair checking a loose shoe on the brown horse. He walked down the lane to the street, and to his surprise saw Clair looking in a shop window. She looked relieved to see him.

'I just saw that man I told you about,' she said. 'He went down the lane to Garcia's stables. I thought there might be trouble if you two ran into each other.'

'There was no trouble. His name is

Hyland and he's a messenger boy for the hide-pirates, but he's pretty sure of himself and too smart to cause trouble here.'

'Mr Waldron is paying me to be his eyes around town, until he can walk properly again. I am supposed just to keep my eyes and ears open and report anything unusual to him.'

'Be very careful,' Notso warned. 'Don't let anyone know what you are up to because there is almost certainly one murderer loose in this town and maybe even more. Don't get too close to some of the suspicious characters. They can be very dangerous.'

Clair smiled. 'Notso, you are starting to sound like an old mother hen. I don't intend to take any risks.'

'That's real nice to hear.'

*　*　*

Big Jim looked at the copied message before him and glared back at the nervous Western Union operator. 'When did you get this?'

The man swallowed nervously, then replied, 'It came through from Woodville this morning. You said you wanted to see any stuff like this.'

Hardiman fished a dollar from his pocket and flipped it to the telegraphist. 'Thanks, John. I can use this. If all goes well I might even pay you a bonus. Tell that to your friend in Woodville too.'

Walking back into the street he called to Andy Cooper, who was waiting near their horses. The younger man's face still bore the marks of his disagreement with the big teamster. 'Andy, start rounding up the boys. There's a big job coming up.'

'Do you want them all? There's a couple of them away somewhere, probably drunk.'

'That's their bad luck. They'll miss out on a nice little payoff but we're better off without drunks. I want at least half a dozen as well as you and me. Find them one at a time and tell them I want to see them. Don't talk to anyone you don't need to.' As an afterthought he added, 'Best get Bill Somers to start overhauling the wagon and harness. I reckon we might need it.'

★   ★   ★

Notso had finished work for the day and was having a quiet drink in the saloon when Gus Saunders joined him.

'Just the man I was after,' the deputy said. 'Do you have a few minutes to talk?'

'I have but it might be an idea to go somewhere quieter if it's something important.'

'It might be safer to talk here if we keep our voices down. I don't want folks to think that you and I are plotting something.'

Notso took another sip of his drink and asked quietly, 'What's on your mind?'

Saunders looked around and seeing nobody close by, muttered out of the side of his mouth, 'It's that Ennis shooting. I'm not sure if it was a plot to get me or just a clumsy attempt at a jail break.'

'Who would want to kill you, Gus? A lot of threats against lawmen are made by dissatisfied customers, but that goes with the job. Do you have a special enemy?'

'I might have but I'm not sure who it is. It could be the sheriff or Jack Carter or even both.'

'Any idea why? That's a pretty serious accusation.'

'Helmer is forever writing letters and I think that secretly he could be tipping off those hide-pirates as to our every move. He always makes some excuse when I suggest we start moving against them.'

'What about Carter?'

'That sour sonofabitch wants to step into Heimer's shoes when he retires. He sees me as a rival for the job. Someone gave Ennis that gun, someone who knew I would be on guard. It was only luck that Ennis misjudged things. He had to stick the gun through the cell door. I had room to move and was able to get my gun out quicker.'

'You were lucky there. Not too many will take that risk when a man has the drop on them.'

'I had nothing to lose. That sonofabitch would have shot me anyway when I let him out of the cell. He had two chances but missed because I moved to an angle where he couldn't move his gun arm properly on account of it being through the bars. But I'm not worried about Ennis. It's what's likely to happen in our office that has me worried. I know something is in the wind and that I am not part of it. I'm asking you and Waldron to watch my back because I think I am a marked man. If I see anything suspicious, I'll pass it on to you and if you find out something that might affect me, for God's sake let me know.'

'I'll tell Sam about this little talk,' Notso promised. 'He's not the type who will let a man be killed if he can help it. I'm pretty sure he can arrange something that will suit the situation we both seem to be in. But, just while I think of it, do you know a man called Hyland?'

'I sure do. He's a shady character who comes and goes. We know he's up to no good but he behaves himself and there has never been a cause to arrest him. Why do you ask?'

'Is there any chance he could be working for someone in your office as an informant or something like that?'

Saunders thought for a while before replying. 'I know the other two don't tell me much but it's highly unlikely that Hyland was giving them information. He is reputed to work for Big Jim Hardiman and I suspect that he does. I wouldn't trust him an inch. Why would he have a connection with the sheriff's office?'

'That's what I'm rather anxious to find out. I'll get going now. It's best folks don't see us too deep in conversation. I'll pass your message on to Sam.'

15

'Get over to Nicholson's store,' Sam ordered, 'and get yourself one of those '73 Winchester .44/40s and some ammunition. Put it on my account. I have a job for you and it's likely to end in shooting.'

Notso had worked with Sam long enough to know that shooting was much more than likely. 'What do you have in mind?'

'There's a shooting outfit for our client company resting on Crooked Creek. They have come up from the south where the recent rainfall has made the ground too soft for their wagons. They have a big load of hides that they will try to ship by rail from Cannon Flats. But their mules are pretty low in condition so they need a couple of days' rest on good feed. The boss is a man called Albert Mallory. I want you to join him and help keep him out of trouble until more protection can be arranged.'

'I assume that Big Jim knows about this?'

'You can bet your boots he does. He has a few Western Union people in his pocket and I know they pass on information from telegrams to him. Just get to Mallory's camp quickly and keep him on his guard. Help is coming but it could be days away. It is safer to fort up on Crooked Creek than to be caught on the plains.'

'If you know that Western Union operators are wrongly passing on information, why don't you stop them?'

Sam smiled and shook his head. 'You need to be a bit subtle in this game. Not all the information that Big Jim gets will be helpful to him. Now start organizing yourself. I want you gone by daylight tomorrow morning. I'm catching the stage to Cannon Flats tomorrow to fix things on the railroad end.'

Clair had risen early. With one of her aunt's sunbonnets, different clothes and a shopping basket on her arm, she walked out of the house in time to see Notso cantering his black mare out of town. He had not seen her and she made no attempt to attract his attention. Then she saw Hyland emerge from the lane beside the sheriff's office, glance at the distant rider and hurry to the Western Union office. She did not need to be a detective to see that his haste was connected with Notso's departure.

Florence was just opening the office when Clair came hurrying along the boardwalk. Her attitude towards the younger woman had changed slightly since Sam had advised her recruitment on a part-time basis.

'Mrs Gower, will Mr Waldron be in today?'

'No. He caught the stage to Cannon Flats this morning — won't be back for a couple of days. What's the trouble?'

'I saw Notso riding out of town a while ago. I think he's in danger. A man who works for Hardiman saw him and hurried to the telegraph office. Do you know where Notso is going?'

Florence looked cautiously about, then, adopting a conspiratorial tone, she said, 'He's going to a buffalo camp on Crooked Creek, but nobody's supposed to know.'

'He didn't tell anyone at the sheriff's office?'

'I don't know. Why?'

'Because I think Hardiman's man was coming from there. I've seen him hanging about there before. Do you know who's on duty there at present?'

'No, I don't,' Florence admitted. 'That would be fairly easy to find out, but Sam Waldron would not be giving away any important information to our local lawmen.'

'He might have let something slip accidentally. I think I should warn Notso. Does Mr Waldron own a horse I could borrow?'

'His horse is stabled at Garcia's and the company also owns a horse that Notso bought recently. You could borrow that, but are you sure it's necessary?'

'I think someone should warn Notso that trouble is on its way. I'm going to change clothes and collect that horse. I'll check with you again before I go.'

Florence was still doubtful. 'I'm not sure that Mr Waldron would approve. Make sure nothing happens to that horse.'

'I'll look after the horse, but it is easier to replace than Notso is. You might need to keep your eyes and ears open while I'm gone.'

'Young lady, I must remind you that I have worked for this agency for two years, considerably longer than your two minutes. I know what I need to do. Now get that horse and see me before you leave.'

Two hours later Clair was well on the way to Crooked Creek. The bay horse was going well under its unaccustomed light weight and was pleased to be outside, stretching its legs again. Had the situation not been so urgent Clair would have enjoyed the ride, but she had no proper trail to follow and was uncertain where she would find Notso. It was possible to see for miles on the plains, but his horse was a good one and he had a long start.

In the pocket of her skirt was a small .32 revolver that Florence had given her, together with a warning that it was fully loaded and was only to be used as a close-range weapon of last resort. She had given her no spare ammunition. 'If you are not out of trouble by the time you have emptied that gun,' she'd announced with great certainty, 'reloading will not help you.'

Clair was prepared to waste a couple of shots signalling Notso if she saw him, but saw no point in telling Florence that.

★ ★ ★

Big Jim assembled a heavily armed group and started out before dawn broke. He left the wagon to follow a couple of hours later and a rider was left behind to check any information when the telegraph office opened. The man was well-mounted and would catch up with the others before the day was out. The plan was for the hide-pirates to halt overnight and to hit the camp early on the following morning. He had recruited a few extra men and was confident that they outnumbered the shooters and skinners of the buffalo outfit. With the element of surprise, he hoped to have most of his intended victims down before they were fully awake. No potential witnesses were to be left alive.

A couple of Hardiman's new recruits were unknown as far as fighting ability was concerned but they were money-hungry and he knew that greed was a good motivation in his line of work. If they proved to be useless he would be prepared to shoot them himself after the camp was taken. The fewer survivors, the less he had to pay out.

Creek Johnny and the skinny one called Isaac were scouting a mile ahead of the group as they rode south. Big Jim did not like nasty surprises unless he was the one dealing them out.

Notso had made good time, as he was more familiar with the country than he had been before. He could see the distant hills behind Crooked Creek, so he decided to rest Snowball for a while and let her graze on the buffalo grass. He would use the time to eat the small amount of food he had brought from town. He selected a resting spot on a low rise among a few trees, where he had a good all-around view and a degree of concealment.

A thin column of smoke suddenly arose from the direction of the creek; he was prepared to bet that Mallory's cook was preparing the noonday meal. The smoke would be a sure indication of the campsite, so he could ride straight across the plains to where it was located. That was easier than finding the creek and then following wagon tracks.

But Notso was not the only one who saw the smoke. Clair sighted it too and aimed her horse towards it. She guessed she was within a two-hour ride of the camp but had seen no sign of Notso. Espying a small rise and a few trees almost directly ahead, she rode towards it, hoping to sight a tiny dot in the sea of grass that would be the one she sought.

Notso had seen the rider on his back-trail, and as a precaution had taken the Winchester from his saddle. Remaining under cover he watched as the stranger rode closer. Then familiar details became plain. What's Clair doing out here? he asked himself — and riding an agency horse, too? Not wishing to startle her, he let Clair get closer before emerging from cover and waving his hat. 'Over here, Clair.'

She cantered across to him and Notso asked when she halted, 'What are you doing out here? Did Sam send you?'

'I'm so glad I found you, Notso. Mr Waldron is away but I came to warn you. I think Big Jim is planning to send men out here. His messenger was in town and I saw him go to the telegraph office when you rode out of town. He was in a hurry. I thought you should know to expect trouble.'

Notso chose his words carefully, so that he sounded concerned rather than reproachful. 'Sam told me to expect trouble but it don't look like he told you. It was nice of you to come all the way out here to warn me, but it has left you in a bad spot. If you try to go back to Woodville, you might run into Hardiman's men. For safety's sake I think you ought to come with me to the buffalo camp, but even that might not be too safe soon. I'll have to find you somewhere that's away from stray bullets because if all goes to plan, there will be plenty of lead flying about.'

'Don't worry about me. Florence

gave me a gun and told me how it works. I can look after myself.'

'Any gun you're carrying is not going to have much range or hitting power. If Big Jim's men get close enough for you to use it, we will be in a heap of trouble.'

'What's this all about, Notso?'

'Sam didn't tell me all the details but I reckon we are the bait in a trap. Our job is to delay Big Jim's men until Sam arrives with reinforcements. He don't know when that will be but every minute we delay them it will be harder for them to get away with the loot.'

'But what will happen to us?'

Notso could find no words to soften the impact of his message. 'If they get the hides it will be because we are dead. Hardiman's gang don't leave witnesses behind.' He paused, looked around and pointed. A small dot was moving across the distant plain. 'Time we were moving, because I reckon that's a scout headed our way.'

16

The Creek snapped shut his small brass telescope. Like all Indians he had been quick to embrace any technology that gave him an advantage in hunting or warfare. He thought he had spotted movement on the distant hill to the south and the telescope had confirmed his suspicion. Two riders were disappearing over the crest and one was on a coal-black horse that he was sure he had seen before. He could not see much detail about the riders but the partially healed wound on his leg reminded him of a previous meeting with the man on the black horse. He could say for certain that both riders were headed for Mallory's buffalo camp, but he had no idea of their intentions. Like a good scout, he would report what he had seen and leave others to evaluate his information.

He had separated from Roy a couple

of hours previously, sending his younger companion further up the creek to make sure no other hunters were in the area. Each would return to Big Jim's camp by a different route.

He found Big Jim and his men a few miles to the west on the upper reaches of Crooked Creek. It was a place where the gang would assemble if they were arriving from various places. They dared not risk a campfire and, in lieu of coffee, were passing around a whiskey jug.

Hardiman was seated on a saddle blanket with his back against a cottonwood tree. 'Come over here, Johnny,' he invited, 'and tell me what you've been up to. What's happening at Mallory's camp?'

'I saw two riders headed that way, so I reckon Mallory has a couple of extra guns. If he has, he has probably been warned. The camp has not moved. By the smoke, it's still on the creek.'

Big Jim scratched his stubbled chin and thought awhile before asking, 'How many guns do you reckon are in that camp?'

'With those new ones, maybe six or

eight. The sides could be pretty close to even and that's not good when they know we're coming. You can bet they'll be watching for anyone coming from the direction of Simpsons Creek. We could be walking into a hornets' nest.'

'I ain't that dumb. We'll do a big circle around the camp and come in from the downstream side. They're sure to be watching in the wrong direction.'

Reaching into his vest pocket, Hardiman produced a silver star. Theatrically he breathed on it and polished it on his shirtfront before pinning it to his vest. 'You're looking at a genuine lawman. We ride in at dusk and I'll announce that I have been sent to put an end to camp raiding. Then, as soon as they put down their guns, we start shooting. With surprise on our side, they won't have a chance.'

It was the hatchet-faced gunman called Isaac who disagreed. 'There's a problem with that idea, Jim. You're better known than most of us and are a sort of distinctive shape. Someone in that camp might recognize you. I think

172

we need someone else to play the lawman and you to keep in the background.'

'He's right,' Roy agreed.

'I could pretend to be the lawman,' Andy Cooper volunteered.

'You ain't old enough.' Hardiman was about to add that he was not smart enough either but decided it was best to keep the young killer's loyalty at least till the job was done. Instead he suggested, 'I reckon Roy should wear the star. With that big voice of his, he sounds like a lawman and he ain't very well known around these parts.'

*　*　*

Clair and Notso had no trouble locating Mallory's camp but the shooter was most unhappy when he saw that one of his much-needed reinforcements was a woman. Even though a black beard covered part of his expression, his eyes showed his disapproval of the situation.

After scowling through their introductions, the shooter asked, 'Where are all the others? Sam Waldron was supposed to send enough men to get us safely to the railhead. There's hide-stealers around these parts.'

Notso could only say, and hope he was right, that help was coming. In Clair's defence he said that she had taken a considerable risk to warn of impending trouble.

After that Mallory cooled down slightly. He explained that he had six men, counting himself, and had heard that the hide-thieves attacked in large groups. The camp, with three wagons and a collection of horses and mules, would be hard to defend. He had decided to let the stock loose as they would only be slaughtered in the crossfire if confined in the camp.

It was then that Notso made his suggestion. 'What if we get Clair to herd the stock well out on the prairie? It will keep her out of harm's way and save our animals. If things go really bad, she has a chance to get away.'

'Do you know about herding, young

lady?' Mallory asked.

'I've done it before when we were moving West, I have a good horse and it has probably done its share of ranch work.'

Mallory allowed himself a smile. 'Miss Hall, you have just got yourself a job.'

'I'd rather help defend the camp,' Clair insisted. 'I have a gun.'

'You might still have to use it,' Notso told her. 'But pray that you don't. If you think the camp is being overrun, get out of here. A few shots from a pistol won't make any difference then.'

'Hang your horses up to one of the wagon tailgates,' Mallory invited, 'then come and get some grub. It could be a long night.'

The new arrivals were soon hungrily devouring plates of buffalo stew while Mallory told them all he knew. It was not much. A US marshal named Heffron had persuaded him to ship his hides from Cannon Flats. Heffron was leading a coordinated investigation aimed at stamping out hide piracy and corruption in the telegraph system.

Notso could add little to the information but guessed that Sam Waldron had also been officially invited to join the operation.

Clair said little, speaking only when spoken to directly. In her mind she was rehearsing the role she would have to play. She would be alone with the loose stock far from the camp. The recall signal would be three evenly spaced shots and she would drive the animals back to the camp. But if she did not hear them after the shooting had stopped, she was to abandon her charges and ride hard for Woodville.

'Your horses have come a long way,' Mallory said. 'Let them go with our stock. Miss Hall can ride a split-eared buffalo pony that I traded from the Utes. He is smart and gentle and has herding stock down to a fine art.'

'You might need to put out a sentry or two,' Notso reminded.

The shooter laughed. 'I'm two jumps ahead of you there. My best shooter,

Josh Lacey, is scouting up the creek for a couple of miles. We reckon them skunks will be coming from the north-west and staying in the timber along the creek. Josh used to scout for the army and he'll see them coyotes before they see him.' Then turning to Clair, he said, 'It might be an idea if you take a rest on my bedroll; it's the one over there by that biggest wagon. You look done in. Herding can be monotonous and if you are tired enough you could fall asleep.'

Clair did not want to miss anything that was happening and declared, 'I won't go to sleep. I hear a lot of stories but don't believe people can sleep on horseback.'

'They certainly can,' Notso told her. 'Sleep creeps up on you and next thing you know, you get a falling feeling if the horse changes direction. You don't fall off but it feels as though you are. You get a very nasty scare. Get some rest while you can. I'll call you when you are needed.'

Reluctantly, Clair retired while Notso tended to their mounts. Mallory brought a wiry little pinto pony and cinched the girl's saddle on its back. 'This little mustang is a hell of a lot better than he looks. The lady should be as safe as she could be on him. My horses and mules are used to being herded but there's one mean old grey mule might need a bit of watching. He hangs back and tempts the herder to ride closer and then lashes out with both heels.'

'I'll make sure I warn Clair about that one,' Notso promised.

Mallory had arranged his wagons in a rough triangle to shelter the camp as much as possible, but there were still gaps that mounted men could pass through and the trees along the creek gave ample shelter for anyone using a stealthy approach. It was not a strong defensive position but at least the camp was not wide open as Joe Long's had been.

The sun was setting when Josh Lacey returned to camp. He came in at a gallop on a foam-covered horse. 'They're comin'. I didn't wait till they was close enough to count but there's a big bunch of riders comin' from the north-west.'

'How far away are they?' Mallory demanded.

'Unless they speed up, we've got maybe half an hour.'

'Looks like they'll hit us just after dark,' Notso observed. But then he had another thought. 'I wonder if it's the lawmen who are expected? We don't want to shoot up the wrong bunch.'

'That's right,' Mallory agreed. 'If it is the law, though, they ain't likely to be sneaking up on us.'

'I'll get Clair out with the livestock and keep them out of harm's way. She will be safer there than here in camp.'

Though he hated waking her, Notso tapped the sleeping girl on the shoulder. 'Time to get up, Clair. Trouble's coming and we need you to hold the stock. Mallory has a fresh pony for you.'

Clair rubbed her eyes and sat up quickly. 'I'd rather stay in the camp.'

'You'll be doing a mighty important

job. Those animals will be needed to shift everything later. If they are kept in camp, half of them could be shot in the crossfire. Now while you are getting ready to ride I'll get you a whip from Mallory.'

'I don't need a whip.'

'Yes you do. Mallory was warning me about a mean old grey mule that will kick the herder if it gets the chance. These old rogues will stand until you ride close enough and then try to kick you. Some of them will run backwards to get a good kick at you, so don't ride too close. If he plays any tricks flick the whip at him but stay out of range. When you get on your pony I'll start letting the stock off the picket lines.'

Clair rose and put on her hat. 'You be careful, Notso. Don't get yourself shot.'

'I've always managed to avoid that before, so I've had plenty of practice. Remember, when the shooting stops, listen for three single shots.

'And if you don't hear them, start riding and don't stop.'

17

Big Jim was not quite sure where he was but was confident with Creek Johnny's guidance. It was dark and he could see nothing in the way of landmarks. Crooked Creek was somewhere on his left and he wanted to give it a wide berth in case the men in Mallory's camp heard their horses. They were halted while their scout went ahead to locate the camp. All their planning would be wasted if they went to the creek too soon and emerged on the north-western side of the camp, a direction from which they were expected. They would take a wide detour which Hardiman planned would bring them behind the defenders, but they had to cross the creek at the right place.

All smoking or talking was forbidden lest their presence should be detected as they waited for their spy to return.

Hardiman did not know how the scout would find them in the featureless darkness, but he was confident that he would. His men were not so sure but no one dared utter a word.

He could only guess at the time because Big Jim was unable to read his watch and the minutes seemed to stretch into hours. He was beginning to think something might have happened to Creek Johnny when a horse snorted and a slightly darker shape emerged from the gloom.

'Jim?' The question came in a whisper.

'Over here, Johnny,' Hardiman answered softly. 'What's the news with Mallory and the others?'

'I found 'em. They're on the creek. You can't see their campfire because of the trees but they're only about a mile away. They're suspicious and have moved their stock out onto the prairie away from the camp. There's one guard in the trees near the camp. They probably figure we'll come that way. If we get real careful we can catch 'em lookin' the wrong way.'

'We'll need to be extra careful because that Wise bastard would have warned them. He's in the camp somewhere. I want you to steer us clear of the camp to a place about half a mile downstream. Then we cross the creek, creep up through the timber, and hit the camp from behind. There's fifty bucks in it for you if you want to scout a bit ahead of us and clear out any guards who happen to be in the trees. Can you do that quietly?'

Creek Johnny's white teeth flashed in the darkness. 'Have your fifty bucks ready, Jim, because any poor sonofabitch in those trees is as good as dead.'

* * *

Notso was uneasy. The expected attack had not come and he was now convinced that the hide-bandits planned a stealthy approach. Their most logical route would be through the trees that lined the creek bank. Mallory had posted one of his shooters there to guard against a surprise attack from that quarter, a middle-aged man with a reputation for straight shooting. Ed Griffin had been through the civil war and was no stranger to sentry duty. But Griffin had made one mistake.

He was facing upstream in the direction of the approaching riders. Creek Johnny's left arm locked around his mouth from behind and a stab to a kidney paralysed him. The only sound the sentry made was when his throat was slashed and his body collapsed on the ground. Pausing only to rifle the dead man's pockets, the killer was ready to slip away. The way was now clear for Big Jim's men to advance through the timber and attack the unsuspecting camp from behind.

'They're taking their time getting here,' Mallory whispered to Notso. Both men were cradling their rifles in their arms as they peered around the end of a wagon.

Before Notso could reply a horse

snorted somewhere in the distance. The sound was faint and had carried a long way through the silent prairie night, but it was unmistakable.

'It could be just a band of mustangs coming in to water,' the hunter said hopefully, even though he regarded the possibility as wishful thinking.

'Could be,' Notso agreed. 'But it might also mean that those hide-pirates have left their horses and are creeping up on foot. Keep your eyes open here. I'm going to warn your man in the trees. He might be the first to see them.'

Pausing only to whisper a warning to another couple of men crouched by a wagon, Notso made his way silently to where Griffin had been posted. Suddenly he discerned a dark shape moving through the trees only feet away from where he stood. He knew it should not have been the sentry but had to make sure. 'Is that you, Griffin?'

The question brought no words but a flurry of activity. The dark shape suddenly lunged towards him.

Instinctively Notso parried an unseen thrust with the barrel of his rifle and heard the rasp of steel on steel. Then he followed through with a butt stroke that connected solidly with the figure before him. The assailant collapsed without a sound but Notso was taking no chances. With all his strength he drove the iron-shod rifle butt downwards at the fallen man. He did not see exactly where it landed but the jarring impact told him the blow's recipient would be out of action.

'What's going on over there?' Mallory called when he heard the violent movement among the trees.

Notso kept his voice low in the hope that none of their enemies was close enough to hear. 'They're here. One got Griffin, but I got him. Get ready.'

'Where are they?' Mallory could not conceal his anxiety as he looked about him into the darkness. 'Are they upstream of us or downstream?'

'I don't know. Those riders we heard upstream might have looped around us on the other side of the creek where we couldn't see them. They might even have split up and could hit us from both sides. This is one fight we have to figure out as we go.'

★ ★ ★

Half a mile downstream Hardiman said quietly to his men, 'It's time to go. Johnny would have silenced any guards they have out now.'

'How do we know the guards didn't get him?' Hyland asked.

'Because we would have heard the shouting and shooting from here. Mallory and his men would be feeling downright nervous. They'd shoot first and ask questions later.' Big Jim paused, then called softly, 'Roy. Come up here. You are appointed a lawman and need to do the first bit of talk to get us into the camp. You will need a name to identify yourself. Can you think of one?'

Roy thought for a while. 'There was one mean sonofabitch in Texas, a US marshal named Henry Robinson. That's who I'll be. I never had much use for any lawmen, least of all him, but it would be nice to see his ugly face if he found out that we were using his name.'

'Do we ride in shooting or walk in?' Andy Cooper asked. He was keen to add a few more notches to his gun.

'We ride in quietly,' Hardiman told him. 'Roy will talk our way into Mallory's camp. Keep your guns out of sight but have them handy when I give the word. I want them to be over their suspicion and relaxing before we start shooting. Get close to your man and when I say 'Fire', don't leave anyone alive, least of all that skunk called Wise.'

★ ★ ★

'I can hear horses,' one of Mallory's skinners whispered. He pointed down-stream.

Notso moved behind a tree in the timber beside the creek, hoping to catch the attackers in crossfire from the other flank. He listened and heard several horses approaching at a walking pace.

The oncoming horsemen were taking their time and making no effort to move quietly.

One of Mallory's men raised a rifle to his shoulder and peered into the gloom. 'Be careful,' his boss warned. 'There's a few lawmen coming to help us. This could be them. Don't shoot unless they start first. It don't sound like they're trying to creep on us.'

Soon the riders were close enough to be visible as a dark patch in the shadows of the trees. At about forty paces from the wagons they halted.

'Hello the camp,' a voice called. 'Is this the Mallory outfit?'

'It is. Who wants to know?'

'I'm a US marshal with a team of deputies. I hear there's a few hide-stealers around. We're here to see that you get your hides to the railhead and that you don't get any unwelcome visitors.'

Mallory was relieved but still cautious. 'Who are you?'

Roy answered immediately. 'I'm Marshal Robinson and I have a badge to prove it. Just be careful with those guns and I'll come in and show you.'

It was then that Notso called from his place among the trees, 'Are you Henry Robinson from down Texas way?'

'I am.'

Notso's rifle roared and spat a tongue of red flame as the shadowy rider was knocked from his saddle.

'Like hell you are!' Notso called as he worked the loading lever of his Winchester and fired another shot into the milling group of horsemen.

18

In seconds the camp fell into utter confusion. Big Jim's men had not had time to locate the defenders' positions. Though they were the more prepared of the two groups, the hide-pirates mostly lacked targets until the hunters started shooting. Then they could only fire at gun flashes. Those at the rear of the group could not fire because of their comrades in front. Some riders surged forward, hampering those in front who were trying to turn their mounts out of the battle.

One horse took a solid hit with a buffalo rifle and reared straight over backwards, narrowly missing falling on others as it spilled its rider among the churning hoofs.

The defenders fired indiscriminately into the dark, wheeling mass before them, knowing that their shots had a good chance of doing damage.

As Notso had been the closest and his rifle flash the first one seen, several shots came his way, but he had taken the precaution of standing behind the trunk of a large cottonwood. A couple of bullets thudded into the tree and one peeled off a strip of bark just above his head, but none found their intended target.

Roy was down but not out of the fight. When knocked from his saddle he had lost his rifle, but managed to draw his revolver and though half-stunned by a sudden rush of pain, he began firing at a man he could just discern near the end of a wagon. His second shot dropped his target.

'Rush 'em!' Big Jim bellowed from the rear and reinforced his order by forcing his mount against those who hesitated in front. The horse collided with Cooper's animal, causing it to panic and rush through the gap between two wagons.

Mallory was reloading his single-shot

rifle when the charging horse hit him and sent him flying. Winded, he rolled under the wagon as the shot Cooper fired plucked at his trouser leg.

One of the buffalo skinners fired point blank at the young gunman, then saw him drop his gun and slump forward. As the frightened horse spun away, Cooper tumbled to the hoof-torn ground.

Notso heard Big Jim yelling at his men and fired at the dark shape that he suspected was the hide-pirate, but the man appeared to be unscathed. Before he could shoot again a shot from behind him hit the tree just near his head. A displaced piece of bark hit his face and he turned to see a dark shape staggering towards him.

Creek Johnny, his jaw broken and his right shoulder smashed, had rejoined the fight. Only the fact that the 'breed had to shoot left-handed saved Notso. Making unintelligible sounds of rage, Creek Johnny swayed on his feet, full of fight but fatally slow.

Notso fired his rifle from the hip, knocking down his man, but then the firing-pin fell on an empty chamber. Dropping the rifle, he drew his Colt. Simultaneously both antagonists swapped shots.

Only Notso's bullet found its mark and the choking noises from the fallen man ended abruptly. This time Creek Johnny really was out of the fight.

The defenders had taken shelter and were firing at bigger targets from much more stable positions. Their shots were thudding into the hide-bandits, hitting horses and emptying saddles. The element of surprise had been lost along with any cohesion that the attackers may have possessed.

Hyland shouted to Isaac, 'We ain't winning this — I'm going.'

Big Jim had already reached the same conclusion and wheeled his horse out of the cloud of dust and powder smoke away from the fight from where his men were starting to retreat. He did not attract attention by firing his gun, and in the darkness he slipped away, using the wagons for cover. He was just in time.

Another group of riders came galloping from upstream of the creek, shouting as they came and throwing a crescent-shaped cordon around the camp. A voice roared from one of the newcomers. 'Cease firing and stay where you are. I'm US Marshal Arnold Heffron. My men will shoot anyone who points a gun at us. Where's Mallory?'

'I'm here, under the wagon. Be careful. There's still a few of those murdering bastards around here.'

Only Hyland and Isaac were still on their horses. Both men put spurs to their mounts and headed for the open prairie, seeking to break out of the cordon.

Isaac raced between two riders but the speed of his horse did not save him. He passed too close to a man with a shotgun and took a full charge of buckshot that spilled him from his saddle.

Hyland did not take the risk. He held

up his hands and shouted, 'I surrender. Don't shoot.'

One of Mallory's enraged men took a shot at him anyway but missed in the bad light.

'Stop shooting, damn you,' the marshal roared. 'I want that man alive.' Then he ordered Hyland, 'Get off that horse and put your hands up. One wrong move and I'll kill you myself. Mallory, bring out your men so we know who's who.'

Warily the buffalo hunters emerged from cover and stood in a group. Their boss did a quick count. Two men were missing. He knew that Griffin was dead but a skinner called McCoy was not with the survivors. 'Where's McCoy?' he demanded.

'He's dead over there by the end of that wagon,' a man replied. 'He got a bullet through his head.'

'Is anyone wounded?' Heffron asked as he holstered his gun and rode closer.

'Not unless bein' scared counts as a wound,' one of the shooters told him. 'I don't like targets that shoot back and their hides ain't worth a damn thing.'

Notso introduced himself and told Heffron, 'We were expecting you earlier.'

The marshal dismounted and clapped a pair of handcuffs on Hyland as he replied, 'We got delayed. We caught one of Hardiman's wagons headed this way. It had a yellow wheel that we had been told about. A couple of my men are holding it where we can pick it up tomorrow. The driver is chattering away like a parrot, giving us all sorts of information in an effort to save his skin.'

Notso looked around. Where was Big Jim?

'Did anyone see Hardiman? I don't see him among those dead men.'

Mallory suggested, 'He probably crawled off into the trees. We won't find him in the dark unless he's already dead or badly shot up.'

'If he's still on a horse he's getting further away every second we stay here talking,' Notso reminded them. 'I'm going to call in our horses. We can't let

that murdering sonofabitch get away.'
He walked clear of the camp and fired
three evenly spaced shots into the air.

★   ★   ★

Clair had been waiting anxiously since
the time the shooting had stopped. She
had tried to keep her imagination in
check but was haunted by the thought
that the hide-pirates might have pre-
vailed. It seemed ages before she heard
the three shots that signified all was
well. Greatly relieved, she gathered up
her reins and circled around the grazing
stock, moving them into a tighter bunch.
Just in time she remembered the grey
mule who had positioned himself on the
outside of the herd and was glancing at
her over his shoulder as she approached.

Clair flourished the whip that Mallory had given her. 'You old devil,' she
scolded. 'If you come in reach of this
whip, I'll use it on you.'

From somewhere between herself
and the camp, the girl heard a horse

approaching. 'Sounds like Notso's coming out to help me,' she said to the pony as she started the loose animals toward the camp. It was easy to see now, because lanterns had been lit and someone had built up a large fire.

★   ★   ★

Big Jim knew something was wrong with his horse before he had gone a hundred yards from the scene of the fight. It was strangely unresponsive and even when goaded into a shambling canter by heavy use of the spurs, it had an unbalanced, rolling gait. It was obvious that the animal had collected a bullet during the skirmish and it was getting weaker. The rider cursed his luck, because fleeing out onto the open range would leave him few places to hide when his mount gave out and daylight came.

Then he spied a dark mass in the gloom ahead and remembered the stock from the camp, which had been moved out of harm's way. He knew there was a herder with them but that would prove no problem. He could even save a bit of time by taking the herder's horse instead of catching a new mount.

Clair had started the stock moving at a steady walk when she suddenly found them being turned in another direction. She was about to canter her pony around to turn them back when she saw, across the small herd, the dark shape of another rider. Her first impulse was to shout to the stranger that he was in the way, but then she realized that the rider might not be friendly. With her heart pounding, she quietly drew the revolver Florence had given her, but held it close to the pommel of her saddle where it might not be noticed.

Big Jim eased his horse to a walk as he actually sighted the rider herding the stock. It would be easy. He would ride in close on the pretext of coming from the camp, shoot the herder and take his mount.

They were about twenty yards apart when Hardiman called out, 'Don't shoot, partner. I have a message for you.'

Part of Clair's mind wanted to believe that the man was friendly but she knew that her friends in camp would be unlikely to address a woman as 'partner'. She clenched the butt of the revolver tightly, reluctant to leave her charges even though her instincts were shrieking that something was wrong. Should she shoot or just ride hard for the safety of the camp?

The unknown rider came closer. His outline was still indistinct as he rode closer to the stock. Momentarily the dark shape showed up more clearly against the grey mule behind him.

All doubts were dispelled as Clair heard a revolver being cocked.

'Hand over that horse or I'll kill you.'

Something in the rider's menacing tone of voice told Clair that he meant to kill her whether she obeyed his order or not.

She wheeled her pony away and almost over her shoulder, fired a shot in the newcomer's direction.

'You asked for it!' Big Jim snarled.

19

The impact was like a blow from a sledgehammer. First came the numbing shock, then pain ripped through Hardiman's lower leg. The grey mule lashed out again, striking the wounded horse on the shoulder and sending it reeling. Then, as if satisfied with its night's work, the kicker trotted away to join the rest of the stock.

The hide-pirate was totally distracted by the intense pain and felt certain that his leg had been broken. Momentarily he forgot Clair as he struggled to remain in the saddle. Then, in pain and rage, he threw a shot in the girl's direction, but it served no purpose as his target was already lost in the darkness and riding hard for the camp.

Notso had been helping secure a couple of the hide-pirates' loose horses when he heard the shooting.

'Clair's in trouble!' he shouted, and vaulted into the saddle of the horse he was holding. Before his companions had fully realized what was happening, he was picking up his stirrups as he spurred into the darkness.

The animal's former rider was a smaller man than Notso and the stirrups were too short, forcing him to stand uncomfortably high in the saddle to keep in balance with his mount. But that was the least of his worries. He knew that someone was shooting at Clair and instinct told him who the shooter was. It was too dark to see the ground ahead and he could only hope that the horse's night vision was better than his. He heard the stock approaching before he could see them and corrected his mount's course to avoid turning the herd away from the camp.

'Clair!' he shouted. 'Is that you?'

It seemed ages before he heard her voice coming from somewhere behind the stock. 'Notso! Someone's out here shooting at me. He was trying to get my horse.'

Guided by the voice, a much-relieved Notso let the herd run past him and saw the girl riding behind. 'Are you all right?'

'I'm fine. Someone shot at me but he missed. I don't think he's chasing me. It was a couple of hundred yards from here.'

'Keep those horses going right into camp. There's a marshal there who has everything under control. I'll take a ride around and see if I can find who shot at you. There will be more riders here any minute. Tell them to give me a call before they start shooting at anyone. I don't want to get shot by mistake.'

* * *

Big Jim needed no convincing that he was in the worst trouble of his life. Seconds after Clair had galloped away his badly wounded horse finally collapsed. He managed to get clear of the falling animal but there was a searing pain as he tried to put his left foot to the ground. The mule's kick had broken a bone in his lower leg and he fell to the ground in agony. The pain was bad enough but the realization that his career was about to end hurt him nearly as much. He knew that the hunters would soon be on his trail and that, crippled and afoot, he had little chance of eluding them. A quick review of his few options gave him no encouragement; the idea of shooting himself flashed briefly through his mind but he dismissed that notion. He expected to be killed, for he would always resist being captured alive, but the vindictive streak in his nature suggested that he should take with him as many of his enemies as he could. Then his instinct for self-preservation asserted itself.

Instead of fleeing, he would work closer to the camp. Any searchers would not expect him to be moving closer and somehow there was a faint chance that he might even be able to steal a horse. The plan might not work but at least he would try.

Two deputies rode out to assist Notso after Clair had told her story. In the darkness it was impossible to determine the position of her attacker and it was generally agreed that he had ridden away — until a deputy found the dead horse. He called the others.

'That throws a different light on things,' Notso said. 'Looks like our man's on foot. He must still be around here.'

John Price, a middle-aged deputy, had chased more than his share of outlaws in the last twenty years. 'If I was him, I wouldn't be. I'd use these last couple of hours of darkness to get as far away from here as I could.'

'We have him now. He'll be lucky to get six miles and on this open prairie he'll stick out like a sore thumb,' said Jud Lucas, his fellow lawman.

Notso disagreed. 'I think he'll go the other way, to Crooked Creek. There's not a lot of water between here and Woodville. Let's have a ride around and see if we can find him, but we might have to wait till morning to start a decent search.'

Big Jim tried to ignore his injured leg as he dragged himself painfully through the grass. He would lie still when he heard a rider approaching, confident that he would be almost invisible at ground level. No horseman even came close to where he was lying and on the dark, featureless prairie, a systematic search was impossible.

Yard by yard the hide-pirate crawled and wriggled towards the campfire. He heard the searchers talking among themselves and eventually riding back to the camp. His elbows and knees were sore but Hardiman forced himself to keep going. He had a hideout in mind, one of a kind that was fairly common in buffalo country and could be found in places that its name did not suggest. Those who did not know better associated buffalo wallows with low-lying, swampy country, but the bison used some in dry country for dust baths or for rubbing off long winter hair.

Eventually he found what he sought fairly close to the camp: just a saucer-shaped depression about nine feet in diameter and about three feet deep at its lowest point. As hunting pressure had driven the buffalo south, the grass around the rim of the wallow was higher than usual and the depression would only be visible from fairly close range.

Big Jim thankfully crawled over the lip of the wallow and settled down to wait for what the day would bring.

★　★　★

In Mallory's camp the horses and mules had been picketed, guards posted and the prisoners secured.

Marshal Heffron had decided that the dead hide-pirates would be buried near where they fell but the men whom Mallory had lost would be retuned to Woodville.

Clair had turned in under a wagon and Notso was sharing a bottle of whiskey with a few of the others before he too sought a rest.

'We were lucky,' Mallory explained to Heffron. 'I thought those coyotes were genuine when they rode into camp. We were expecting you to come from that direction. Notso spoiled their little surprise though.'

'How did you know they were not lawmen?' Heffron asked.

Notso waited for his last sip of whiskey to stop burning its way down his throat before replying. 'He gave the name of a real lawman I knew well, but Henry Robinson shot himself about six months ago when he was drunk. I was at his funeral when they planted him at a little place down on the Texas border.'

Mallory decided he was not drunk enough to be that sort of danger to himself and poured a bit more whiskey into his tin cup. 'These coyotes weren't acting on their own. What about their friends in town?'

Heffron gave a grim smile before telling them, 'I reckon Old Fritz and Sam Waldron have rounded up most of them. They knew that some Western Union operators were working with the hide-pirates so they had to use the mail service to organize their moves. The US Marshal Service had to be involved as well as investigators from Western Union. It was a big operation and very hard to coordinate. Sheriff Heimer knew one of his deputies was selling him out and didn't know which one, but he sure as hell will know by now.'

'So Fritz Heimer was working away quietly while everyone, including his deputies, reckoned he was just slowing down before he quit.'

'That's exactly what the old fox was up to. Your boss, Sam Waldron, was in on the plan too.'

They talked a little longer. Heffron said that they would bury the dead hide-pirates after daylight and then move the wagons out of the area. They would rendezvous with Hardiman's wagon, which they had captured the previous day. Then lawmen, prisoners and wagons would turn for Cannon Flats.

'Unless you need me,' Notso said, 'Clair and I will ride straight back to Woodville. I stashed a dead outlaw's guns down Crooked Creek a ways and will collect them before heading back. I might keep an eye out for Big Jim along the creek.'

Heffron rose and stretched. 'That's fine by me. We have enough men. Now I'll try to grab some shut-eye.'

Not far away, in pain but exhausted, Big Jim also fell asleep.

★ ★ ★

The camp was astir before sunrise. Mallory's cook, despite the late night, woke early and soon had the fire going. Nobody, except possibly the prisoners, wanted to linger on Crooked Creek. The others were looking forward to the comforts of town with good food and long hours of uninterrupted sleep.

Despite the hard ground, Clair slept well and woke reluctantly when Notso roused her with a cup of coffee and some bacon and beans on a tin plate.

'You'd better eat this quick,' he said. 'With so many people in camp, Mallory is short of eating irons. Wolf this lot down and I'll take the plate and cup back to be washed for someone else. When we get back to Woodville, I'll treat you to a proper meal at the hotel.'

'I might just keep you to that promise,' Clair said as she threw aside the blanket she had been loaned and brushed the hair from her eyes.

The camp was a hive of activity, with those who had eaten harnessing teams, saddling horses and digging graves for the dead outlaws.

By the time Clair was ready to travel Notso was there with their saddled horses. 'We aren't needed here and watching those dead fellas being planted is not my idea of entertainment. Everyone else is going to Cannon Flats but you and I can head straight back to Woodville. I have to make a slight detour to collect some guns I left down along the creek a few days ago, but that won't take long.'

'The sooner we leave this place the better. It gives me the creeps. There has been so much killing here.'

'And there could be more yet,' Notso predicted. 'Big Jim Hardiman could still be around here. In a couple of hours on foot he couldn't have gotten far. We'll need to watch for him while we are on Crooked Creek, even though a couple of Heffron's men have checked it for a mile or so and found no sign of him.'

Big Jim was not on Crooked Creek but he was dreaming of its cool waters. He had been many hours without a drink and knew that even when the lawmen left, he would have a difficult time getting to the water and shade that he now craved.

The sun was beating down despite the early hour and staying in the shadeless buffalo wallow would be an ordeal. He lay there sweating, suffering and cursing silently, waiting for the time when it would be safe to emerge.

At last the hide-pirate heard the rumbling of the wagons and the sound of hoofbeats as his hunters left the camp. Aware that he might be spotted by some straggler, he forced himself to remain where he was, because it would be nearly an hour before the others were lost to sight. Though distressed, Big Jim determined not to be captured as the result of a foolish mistake.

Notso and Clair had left the camp early, both relieved to be away from the scene of such bloodshed. It was pleasant riding in the shade of the trees along the creek, but the thought that Hardiman might be lurking nearby dampened any feelings of relaxation. Notso rode a horse-length ahead on the pretext of finding the way, but he wanted Clair behind him if any shooting started. Despite assurances that Big Jim was not hiding along the creek, he reckoned that the hide-pirate would be less likely to flee on foot across the open prairie and did not accept the idea that he was miles away. Riding Indian-file with a pretty girl might be unsociable but for her it was safer.

It took a while to find where he

had stashed the guns, as originally he had been in a hurry and had paid little attention to landmarks. Eventually though, he recognized familiar surroundings and found the weapons where he had left them.

He checked both revolvers, reloaded them each with five bullets, and left the hammers resting on empty chambers as a safety measure. Then he attached the belt and holsters to the pommel of his saddle. He unloaded the carbine and fed the cartridges back into the magazine leaving the firing chamber empty. As he arranged it on the pommel of Clair's saddle, he told her, 'This can't go off accidentally, but if you should need it, and I hope you don't, just work the lever and the rifle will be ready to fire.'

Clair laughed. 'Do you really think I'll need to shoot my way back to Woodville?'

'I guess not, but I have an aversion to carrying guns that can't be used.'

'Where do we go from here?' Clair pointed across the almost featureless grassland. 'It all looks the same.'

'Easiest way is to follow the creek back to near Long's camp and then ride straight north.'

When Big Jim at last peered over the rim of the buffalo wallow he saw that the hunters were gone. He crawled from his shelter and, painfully dragging his injured leg, took the shortest line to the water. Progress was slow and his hands and good knee were soon raw and bleeding from the small stones and spiky weeds in the grass. But these discomforts were minor compared to his raging thirst.

It seemed ages before he rolled down the sloping bank and thrust his sun-scorched face into the cool water. Though strongly tempted to keep drinking, he had a few mouthfuls then stopped, lest he should find himself crippled by cramps. Glancing around he saw a forked sapling growing nearby; it would make a rough crutch with a few cuts in the right places. He decided to start on that task before returning for another drink.

Even with his sharp pocket knife,

cutting through the base of the sapling was not easy, especially as he was forced to lie on the ground. At last he had weakened the wood to the extent that it broke with a loud crack and he fell back on the sloping bank, jarring his injured leg in the process. He groaned aloud in pain.

'So this is where you got to,' Notso said as, gun in hand, he urged the black mare through the trees.

20

'Don't try reaching for a gun,' Notso warned, 'because you won't make it. And while you're being cooperative you can toss that pocket knife away too.'

Hardiman briefly considered reaching for his gun but decided that his chances of survival would be better with a good lawyer. 'Don't worry. I have no intention of giving you an excuse to shoot me. I won't resist. I think I have a broken leg anyway.'

'Were you shot?'

'A mule kicked me.'

'That's real nice to know. It also explains why you were chopping into that stick like a beaver gone mad. I heard you breaking up the scenery and got a mite curious. Now — unbuckle that gun belt and throw it out of your reach. Be very careful how you do it.'

Big Jim complied, having already

dismissed any notions of resistance. With limited movement he knew he had no chance of beating a man who had the drop on him.

Notso dismounted and, holding his gun close to the prisoner's head, demanded that he should carefully remove any concealed weapons. He added, 'You might not know it but there's two of us here and you are covered by a rifle. Don't try any tricks.'

Carefully removing a Colt derringer from his pocket, Hardiman tossed it a short distance away. At the same time he twisted around enough to see Clair sitting back in the trees with a rifle pointed in his direction. 'That's a girl!' he exclaimed.

'That's right. You took a shot at her last night. You're lucky you missed, otherwise you'd be dead meat. Now where's that other derringer? These little pop-guns are often sold in pairs.'

In the tone of one thoroughly defeated, Big Jim mumbled, 'It's in my left hip pocket. I've got bruises from sitting on the damn thing. I didn't know it was a girl herding those horses last night. I would not have hurt her if I'd known.'

'It's a bit late to pretend to be a gentleman, Big Jim. You wanted a horse and were prepared to kill to get it. Now I want a word with the lady so stay right where you are.'

Clair was still looking down the rifle barrel as Notso backed to where she was. 'What happens now?'

'I want you to ride hard to the wagons and tell the marshal that I have Big Jim and that he has a busted leg so will probably need a wagon. Just follow the creek and you will see where the wagons left camp. The tracks will be easy to follow up.'

'Notso, I don't like leaving you alone with this man. He's very dangerous.'

'The quicker you get help, the less danger I'll be in, so please get going.'

'I'll be as quick as I can,' Clair promised as she wheeled her horse and cantered it out of the trees on to the open ground.

Big Jim listened in silence until the sound of the hoofbeats had faded away. Then he said to Notso, 'Name your price.'

'My price for what?'

'Don't play games with me, Wise. What do you want to put me on that horse and let me go?'

'You haven't enough money to buy me, even if I was for sale. You're a murdering, thieving polecat who would double-cross his own mother, and those are some of your better points.'

'Think well, Wise, because my organization is a big one. The odds are that my men will rescue me and positions will be reversed. Being smart could save your life.'

'I'll let you in on a little secret, Hardiman. The Texas Rangers had an unofficial rule that the prisoner was the first one shot if a rescue was attempted. For your sake, I hope none of your friends comes around.'

Hardiman did not sound worried by Notso's warning. 'You're bluffing, Wise.

Now I'll tell you a secret. I had a big organization going and I doubt that the law will catch them all. We have always planned that any of us escaping should meet here along Crooked Creek. It's a good point to bring the gang back together and there are a lot of directions we can go if we need to keep moving. So I am telling you that some of my men are almost certain to be here before your lady friend can find those lawmen and bring them back. You won't have a snowball's chance in hell when that happens. Sure, you might kill me but you'll be committing suicide at the same time. I can direct you to a thousand dollars in gold if you let me go. Be smart — let me go.'

'I might be called Notso Wise, Hardiman, but I'm not so dumb as to fall for your spiel. Save your breath.'

Hardiman lapsed into silence, which he broke occasionally when the throbbing pain in his leg came in spasms.

Notso was uneasy although he tried not to show it. It was common for outlaw gangs to have an agreed rallying point after they were scattered and Big Jim's organization was extensive. There was a good chance that his prisoner was telling the truth.

An hour passed, then he heard the sound of a horse coming through the timber along the creek bank. Moving cautiously to the cover of a tree trunk, Notso drew a gun.

He told himself that Clair had found the marshal's men and that help was coming, but at the same time he had the uneasy feeling that Big Jim might have been telling the truth.

A rider came through the trees, a familiar figure with a star pinned to his shirt. It was Gus Saunders. He halted his sweating horse when he saw Big Jim on the ground and the black mare nearby. 'Notso!' he called.

'I'm here, Gus.' The detective stepped into the open as he spoke.

'Am I too late?'

'Depends on what you're talking about. What are you doing all the way out here?'

'Sam Waldron asked me to find you. Who's that you have there?'

'That's Big Jim Hardiman. Now why exactly has Sam sent you after me? Don't you work for the sheriff?'

'Not anymore. As of yesterday I've been working for Sam.' As he spoke, Saunders rode closer to Hardiman. Leaning from the saddle, he peered closely at him. 'So this is Big Jim Hardiman. He don't look too big now.'

'Don't get too close to him,' Notso warned. 'What does Sam want to tell me so urgently?'

With his horse screening the movement, Saunders leaned forward, drew a short-barrelled revolver from his boot-top and dropped it beside the prisoner.

Notso saw the movement and swung his gun in a futile attempt to cover both men. Simultaneously Saunders spurred his horse, causing it to bound forward. He was just out of the line of fire when Big Jim took his first shot. The bullet missed but not by much.

Saunders had travelled about thirty

yards before wheeling his horse and jumping from the saddle.

Notso decided that although Big Jim was closer, the deputy was the more dangerous of the two. Forcing himself to ignore the hide-pirate, he turned at right angles and fired at Saunders. His bullet went close enough to make the other flinch and miss the shot he sent in reply. But Notso's position was a bad one, caught in a crossfire by two opponents and with only five shots left in his Colt.

Big Jim was hampered by his injured leg and the short-barrelled weapon. Consequently his second shot missed.

It took a great effort of will but Notso ignored the injured shooter and sighted deliberately on Saunders. The latter, rattled by the sight of a revolver bore pointing straight at him, snapped a quick shot and missed again. He had spoiled his own aim in his haste to avoid the bullet he knew would be coming.

Notso's shot clipped his target's left shoulder, causing him to reel slightly, but he stayed on his feet. Already he was lifting his gun for another shot.

Big Jim had held his fire when he knew that he was not the detective's immediate target. He had four shots left and was watching the duel between the two younger men. He knew that with any luck he might still hold all the aces.

The deputy's nerve broke first. He fired wildly and suddenly his gun was empty. He turned and ran into the trees, seeking a chance to reload. Only then did he realize that his left arm was not working as it should. Reloading was no longer an option. His only thought was to escape. He ran toward his horse but it was one he had stolen when he fled town and it danced nervously away as he tried to approach it.

'Stop!' Notso called. 'Put your hands up.'

Saunders did neither.

Notso's carefully aimed shot hit him in the thigh and spun him around before he fell over.

Rolling onto his back, Saunders brought

up his gun but made no attempt to aim it. Notso was sighting down the barrel of his Colt and, at the range, was unlikely to miss. Suicide held no appeal for the wounded man. He opened his fingers and let the gun fall. 'Don't shoot,' he pleaded.

'This is your lucky day, Gus, but unless you toss that gun as far as you can throw it, that luck is going to end mighty sudden.'

The wounded deputy gingerly picked up the discarded weapon and threw it as far as he could.

'That's real obliging. Now stay there.'

Knowing that his life was hanging by a thread, Saunders had no intention of disobeying.

Notso opened his gun's loading gate, ejected the empty shells and replaced them with live cartridges. 'Try not to bleed to death,' he told the wounded man. 'I'll be back after I settle things with Old Custard Guts over there.'

Hardiman took advantage of the diversion and, ignoring the pain from his injured leg, had dragged himself to the other side of a tree trunk. He had seen how Saunders had lost his nerve and cursed the fact that Notso had emerged from the duel unscathed. He had only three shots and at least one would need to count.

'Throw your gun out, Hardiman. You don't have a chance. Saunders can't help you and you can't get away.'

'If you want my gun, Wise, you'll have to come and get it. I'm waiting for you.'

Aware that he was at extreme range for Big Jim's gun, Notso backed away at a difficult angle for his injured oppo-nent to shoot accurately. Keeping a close eye on the hide-pirate, he worked his way to where he had tethered Snowball. He removed the Winchester carbine from the saddle scabbard and almost casually walked to a point where the tree trunk offered little cover to Big Jim. The gang leader wriggled frantically as he tried to change his position but, even ignoring the agony of his injured leg, he was too slow. Notso's first shot grazed the edge of the tree, splintering wood and tearing bark inches from his target's face. The next one took a toe off the foot that its owner could not withdraw in time.

Made reckless by pain and rage, Big Jim thrust his gun around the tree and tried to sight on his tormentor. A carbine bullet drove bark and wood chips into his face before he could squeeze the trigger. He threw himself back under cover.

'This is your last chance,' Notso called. 'Give up or I'll just keep shooting little bits off you till you drop that gun. You might have some chance in a courtroom with a slick lawyer but you have no chance here. Throw that gun out now because in a second I intend to start shooting and I won't stop until you're dead.'

Suddenly the prospect of a court appearance greatly appealed to Big Jim. He threw his gun away and called, 'I surrender. Don't shoot.'

21

It was a week later and Sam, Notso and the recently retired sheriff of Woodville were having a quiet drink in the agency office. Big Jim and the prisoners had been patched up and transferred to the care of the relevant authorities. Even the paperwork had been grudgingly completed, but Heimer predicted more would be needed when the court proceedings commenced.

'I can't really start to enjoy my retirement until all the court cases are over. It will be nice not having to worry about stopping that hide piracy. That caused me many a sleepless night.'

'That was a tricky business, Fritz,' the detective said. 'It was hard to work knowing that Big Jim was being told of every move we made and having young Saunders in your office made it even harder.'

'I thought I had him covered. I knew from the start that he had killed Ennis and it galled me to let him run as long as he did. And he damn near got away. He saw the federal men grab the Western Union operator and knew the game was up. He just stole the first horse handy and ran for it.'

'He was unlucky that he headed for Crooked Creek,' Notso observed.

Sam smiled knowingly. 'You should remember from your time in the rangers how most outlaw gangs have meeting places where they can come together if they get scattered. Big Jim's men hung about Crooked Creek because it was a long way from people and towns. It was also close to the state line; when they had to run, a short ride put them into another jurisdiction. Fritz can tell you about that. He had the problem for a long time.'

'That's right. Folks were criticizing me for doing nothing, but a premature move would have only tipped our hand. I was writing so many letters that I was sick of it. But it was the only way we could get around Hardiman's spies. He had a lot of people on his payroll.'

'They're all nicely rounded up now,' Sam said.

'That's the trouble,' Heimer growled. 'You could have saved us all a heap of time and paper work, Notso, if you had killed Hardiman and Gus.'

'There were times I tried, Fritz, but my aim wasn't quite good enough, so I settled for taking them alive. Killing people doesn't sit easily with me. Maybe I'm not cut out for this detective game.'

'You're doing just fine,' Sam told him. 'Don't think of quitting on me just when Florence is retiring. I think you will get on very well with her replacement.'

'Why is that?'

'I have just hired Clair Hall. She will be a good addition to our team.'

'Damnit, Sam, you could have saved me a lot of soul-searching if you had told me that earlier. I might be Notso Wise but I sure as hell ain't stupid. I reckon I'll stay around.'

We do hope that you have enjoyed reading this large print book.

Did you know that all of our titles are available for purchase?

We publish a wide range of high quality large print books including:
Romances, Mysteries, Classics
General Fiction
Non Fiction and Westerns

Special interest titles available in large print are:
The Little Oxford Dictionary
Music Book, Song Book
Hymn Book, Service Book

Also available from us courtesy of Oxford University Press:
Young Readers' Dictionary
(large print edition)
Young Readers' Thesaurus
(large print edition)

For further information or a free brochure, please contact us at:
Ulverscroft Large Print Books Ltd.,
The Green, Bradgate Road, Anstey,
Leicester, LE7 7FU, England.
Tel: (00 44) **0116 236 4325**
Fax: (00 44) **0116 234 0205**

GENESIS GUNPLAY

John Davage

Cody McCade rides into Genesis look-ing to uncover the truth about the sudden disappearance of the town's previous sheriff and the mystery of a young man's homestead, razed to the ground just before his wedding. But when up against local thugs and the deadly Shaw family, he realizes it will take more than asking around to get answers. However, the townsfolk have another mystery on their hands: just who is Cody McCade, and what brings him to Genesis?